The Australian

The Australian

a novel

EMMA SMITH-STEVENS

DZANC
BOOKS

**DZANC
BOOKS**

5220 Dexter Ann Arbor Rd.
Ann Arbor, MI 48103
www.dzancbooks.org

Library of Congress Cataloging-in-Publication Data

Names: Smith-Stevens, Emma, 1982- author.
Title: The Australian : a novel / by Emma Smith-Stevens.
Description: First edition. | Ann Arbor, MI : Dzanc Books, 2017.
Identifiers: LCCN 2016038920 (print) | LCCN 2016055287 (ebook) | ISBN 9781941088746 | ISBN 9781945814082
Subjects: LCSH: Young men--Fiction. | Australians--Fiction. | Identity (Psychology)--Fiction. | Self-actualization (Psychology)--Fiction. | Melbourne (Vic.)--Fiction. | New York (N.Y.)--Fiction. | Psychological fiction.
Classification: LCC PS3619.M5975 A97 2017 (print) | LCC PS3619.M5975 (ebook)
| DDC 813/.6--dc23
LC record available at https://lccn.loc.gov/2016038920

First US edition: May 2017
Interior design by Michelle Dotter

Printed in the United States of America

10   9   8   7   6   5   4   3   2   1

For Sebastian

PART ONE

ON THE STREETS OF Melbourne, the Australian parades around dressed as Superman, paying his way through university by posing for photos, conscious of the bulge of his cock. Novelty, sex object, comic relief—it is all good. Radios across his nation have been playing a song that goes, "I've got the brains, you've got the looks, let's make lots of money." In his mind, the Australian is both of the people in the song. He is smart—smart enough to know when effort is absolutely required and when he can fake it—and he is handsome, with chiseled abdominal muscles underneath the chiseled abdominal muscles of his costume. He smiles widely, his teeth luminous, his canines threatening. All his life, he has been indiscriminate with his enthusiasm, invincible within the hedonistic splendor of the present moment, like some kind of inverted Buddha.

This is not to say that the Australian's life has been without adversity. He never had a father, and while his mother means well, her ceaseless affection is like an ill-fitting homemade sweater, all itch and chafe. But these misfortunes are deep in the background, monotonous as a refrigerator's electric hum. They take conscious effort for the Australian to discern—and why bother? His head is filled with sunlight, cricket, mischief, girls. Then, one sunny Friday morning during his last month of schooling, he suddenly acquires for the first time a distinct ambition. As he wraps his right arm around a group of Irish tourists, and as they cram themselves into his sweat-stained armpit, and as he flexes his left bicep, round and stiff as an apple, the Australian thinks: I will be a rich man.

After graduation, the Australian moves to New York to work on Wall Street, but right off the bat, he can't stand his boss. She reminds him of the heartless provocateur who took tickets at the public pool in the seaside town where he spent his childhood summers, who flaunted her tremendous breasts and treated the Australian with what he perceived to be hostile indifference. Day after day, he is unable to focus on the neon river of information that flows from his computer screen— Dow Jones, NASDAQ, symbols, numbers. His attention drifts to the window. Pigeons congregate on a rooftop across the street, and the Australian ponders what diseases they carry, the subtleties of their social order, and how exactly they achieve sexual intercourse. For his inattentiveness and what his boss describes as "failure to demonstrate a sense of urgency," he is reprimanded regularly.

After six months of trying to reckon with his haughty overseer, he quits the brokerage firm and goes to work for himself. He takes the money he has recently inherited from his estranged father, who perished in a rather foreseeable hang-gliding accident, and triples it within eight months through some risky and uncalculated investments. The Australian knows he has struck upon the kind of luck that can turn on you in a heartbeat, that he must take his winnings and move on to some other pursuit.

On a summer afternoon while he is musing over possibilities, the Australian happens upon a coffee shop called Esperanto. A sign in the window reads:

WELCOME * BONVENO

ESPERANTO IS THE UNIVERSAL LANGUAGE OF PEACE AND
UNDERSTANDING. INVENTED IN 1887 BY THE PHYSICIAN
LUDWIG LAZARUS ZAMENHOFF, ESPERANTO IS FREE FROM
ANY NATIONAL, POLITICAL, OR RELIGIOUS AFFILIATION.
"ESPERANTO" MEANS "ONE THAT HOPES."
IT WAS ZAMENHOFF'S HOPE THAT ESPERANTO WOULD
ONE DAY BE THE MOTHER TONGUE OF ALL HUMANKIND.

PEACE * PACO

He thinks of his friends and mother back in Melbourne, and he is submerged in an achy, sloppy feeling. The words *homesick*, *solo*, and *lost* flit through his brain. He wonders whether this feeling is common among expats, and then whether an Australian in New York City can be considered an expat—a word that invokes rough-hewn men in their fifties and sixties playing card games over tequila at tropical beachfront bars. Can a guy in his twenties living in one of the world's great cities, an international hub, be classified among such men? The Australian is disappointed to admit to himself that he is, likely, simply an immigrant.

Reading Esperanto's sign a second time, the idea of a universal mother tongue excites him. "One that hopes" is a description the Australian finds befitting of himself. Perhaps he will learn Esperanto one day. Entering the café, he feels like a citizen of the world.

While sitting in an armchair drinking an iced coffee, he meets a young girl. She is a plump high school student in a tiny red T-shirt and pale blue jeans with ripped knees. She bites her nails in between sips of hot chocolate, a curious choice considering the monstrous heat. The Australian listens to her talk for a long time about how everyone she knows has sold out. When finally she winds down in a way that reminds him of a particular toy from his childhood, he tells her he is a venture capitalist. She follows him home, does some coke with him, spreads her legs.

"What's a venture capitalist?" she asks afterward, sprawled with her limp limbs heavy over his.

He thinks for a moment, distracted by the pain of his knee hyperextending under the weight of her ample thigh, and then says simply: "It takes money to make money."

The girl seems satisfied with that answer.

Henceforth, the Australian tells everyone that he is a venture capitalist.

The Australian swiftly enters the period of his life during which, on Fridays, a dealer named Elijah comes to his apartment with a metal briefcase and sells him an eight ball of coke. It is so pure it makes the Australian's entire face go numb within ten seconds of snorting just one line. Sometimes the Australian asks Elijah to fuck him. Elijah always laughs like it's a joke, and the Australian laughs along with him, although he wants to cry really badly. Usually, after each of these interactions, the Australian goes out and picks up a woman. Eventually one of the women sticks with him—Fiona, a designer of hair accessories and belts. The Australian first meets her during happy hour at an Irish pub dotted with gin-blossomed old men, where he plans to drink the edge off both another pitiful interaction with Elijah and the Colombian cocaine they snorted together. On his walk to the bar, he silently berates himself for having a homosexual attraction and then admonishes himself for feeling ashamed of a desire that he believes should be totally fine. At least, were such a desire to strike another man, he

would not stand in judgment. Can a fellow be sharply averse to thinking of himself as gay, yet not be a homophobe? He cannot reach any
conclusion. Entering the bar with his head hung, he silently swears
that he will quit the whole thing—Elijah's visits and the cocaine—and
it occurs to him that perhaps it is simply Elijah's association with the
narcotic's euphoric effects that kindles the attraction, as opposed to
some deep-seated proclivity. This possibility brightens his mood a bit.

The Australian raises his head and sees a woman seated upon a
barstool. Like a fairy on a flower petal, he thinks. She has strategi-
cally messy short auburn hair, and the pale skin of her face and arms
is lightly freckled. She is not with anyone, nor is she speaking to the
bartender, yet she is smiling a little. As the Australian approaches her,
he is sharply aware that he can't remember when he was last hugged.

"What are you drinking?" he asks.

"A shandy," she says. "Grapefruit juice and beer. It's really good."

"Grapefruit juice? I'll give it a go. Do you mind?" The Australian
points to the barstool beside her.

She shakes her head, and he sits and orders a shandy for himself.
Fiona asks where the Australian is from, and they tumble into a conversation about his relocation to New York two years ago.

"Has it been hard to adjust?" asks Fiona.

"It's tough to meet people," he says, unsure whether he is enact-
ing loneliness as a ploy to reel her in, or whether companionship is
something he really wants.

Fiona talks about leaving the Chicago suburb where she grew up
to attend the Fashion Institute of Technology on a full scholarship,
six years ago now. "My family was dead set against me leaving," she
says. "They wanted me to be a townie, go to community college for
phlebotomy."

"What's—"

"A person who draws blood. A professional vampire, basically."

The Australian thinks of his mother, who always hoped he would be an artist, teacher, or musician—professions she thought would put him in service to humanity. When he announced his plan to work on Wall Street, proclaiming that he would make "buckets of money," his mother sobbed. Later she raged, which he had never seen her do before, using phrases like "capitalist hogs," "plague on your spirit," and "razor-fanged piranhas." The Australian loves his mother and feels guilty for leaving her alone in Melbourne; but more than that, he is glad to be outside the reach of her adoration, which always made him feel pressured—to please her, to stand by her as she cycled through various jobs and men, and to love her in the particular way she understands, which requires a closeness that now seems to him borderline incestuous. His mother slides back into the darkest region of his psyche, where all of the things over which he believes himself to be powerless reside.

Fiona tells him that her first couple years in the city were rough, but she eventually adjusted.

"How?" asks the Australian, embarrassed by the urgency of his tone.

"It just took time." Fiona shrugs. "At first I was terrified, but eventually that turned to excitement, still with some nervousness, though, and then one day—literally, I just woke up one morning, and I was happy here. Even my body felt strong, like in those stories about mothers who suddenly have the strength to lift a car or fallen tree or whatever massive thing threatens their babies' lives—not that I have a baby."

The Australian nods, although he doesn't quite follow.

"Well, I guess I was my own baby," Fiona continues. "I came out from under my fear, and my guilt for leaving my family, and holy shit—I was living in New York City, I was studying fashion design at one of the best schools in the world, I'd made some awesome friends, and I hadn't even realized it. Not *really*. I wondered if I was going crazy or if I was finally waking up, and so I thought, 'Give me a sign.' It was like a prayer, except I'm an atheist. I remember the moment exactly. I was in the living room of my old apartment, cutting my former roommate's hair, and I thought, 'Give me something. Show me this is really happening.' And I looked out the window and there was a triple rainbow in the sky."

Fiona initially claims to like being spanked, which turns out to be a lie. She lies about a lot of things. Not typical things like age and hair color, but strange things like what time she woke up or whether or not she likes papaya. The triple-rainbow story, she confesses, was a fabrication, too—"But a good one!" she says, and the Australian must admit it is true. She has interesting friends and lives in a relatively spacious, rent-controlled apartment. She is not just surviving the city, she is flourishing in it. The Australian keeps her around because he feels elevated by her presence. Also, she is very affirming. "I wish you could see yourself like I do," she says. "You really are incredible."

Five months after they begin dating, Fiona suggests she and the Australian move in together. "You're here, like, six nights a week," she says while making goat cheese and tomato omelets in her kitchen.

The Australian feels certain he only spends two or three nights at her apartment each week, tops. He thinks more carefully and realizes, with some apprehension, that she is correct. "Living together—that's a big deal," he says. "I've got to think about it."

Sitting on a stool at the kitchen island, he shuts his eyes. He has never lived with a girlfriend before. He feels at ease in Fiona's home, more comfortable than he feels in his own. He wonders whether this is because Fiona's apartment is charming and cheap while his is barren and expensive. Yes, he concludes, but there is more to it. She never criticizes him or tries to change him. She views him as good-hearted, intelligent, and adult, which sometimes makes him anxious, but mostly just feels nice. Being with her has forced him to bulldoze his way into venture capitalism, lest she discover he deceived her about his job at their first meeting. He has networked, forged a few connections, partnered with some guys to get a couple startups off the ground—one that makes virtual patients for nursing students to practice interviewing, another that manufactures cars that run on algae. He has yet to make any real money, but he figures it's only a matter of time.

More importantly, the Australian realizes that he loves being loved, particularly the way Fiona loves him: simply, tenderly. He would be a fool to say no to a woman whom—yes, he is sure—he loves back. He loves her laugh, her buzzing energy, her lies. Also, the sex is fantastic. The Australian had exciting sex with a couple women during university, plus a few top-notch flings in New York, but he was never able to sustain interest for longer than a month or two until now. For this, Fiona deserves credit. He opens his eyes. There is an omelet steaming on the kitchen island in front of him.

"I want to live here with you," he says. "That sounds perfect."

The Australian's foray into venture capitalism is brief. Despite what seemed like a promising start, he has a difficult time getting investors of any real means to partner with him. It is a misfortune he can't make any sense of, although he doesn't really try, because he is not one to dwell in mystery. Instead, he puts his efforts into an idea that comes to him as if by magic one evening as he is smoothing the calluses on his heels with a pumice stone. Along with a business acquaintance from his Wall Street days—a middle-aged woman with hair straightened by a highly toxic Brazilian method, who is constantly trying to get other women to straighten their own hair by the same method—the Australian opens a club. The club is called Day Club. Complete with darkness, booze, and *unce-unce* techno, it is open from eight in the morning until five in the afternoon.

At first, the hottest party kids in the city come, twenty-somethings with trust funds and pronounced cheekbones and ecstasy holes in their brains. When the time comes to renew his immigration visa, the Australian does so without incident. He is making good money, has employees, pays taxes. A lush red carpet to a Green Card seems to be rolling out in front of him. However, the club soon hits a downturn and becomes all high school kids, greasy-haired ravers pressing their bony bodies against the velvet ropes, waving fake IDs at the bouncer. Within a year and a half of opening, Day Club is raided by the city, loses its liquor license, and goes out of business. New York City has no more ideas for him, and he is twenty-eight, and he doesn't want to go back to Australia.

"Why would you go back?" asks Fiona, when the Australian voices his worries.

They are sitting together on the living room couch, watching a thunderstorm roll over the city. Fiona has just been hired as an accessory stylist for a major pop star, whose former stylist was axed for making her look "middle-aged"—never mind that the pop star is forty-six.

"I can take care of us for a while." She kisses his cheek and neck, rests her head against his chest.

The Australian's heart begins thumping irregularly. He wonders if he is experiencing a life-threatening cardiac event, and then he realizes that he is about to ask Fiona to marry him. Some drive is pushing him toward proposing, a need even greater than his desire to remain in the United States. It must be love. What else could it be, this invisible force squeezing his ribcage?

The Australian takes her hands and rests his forehead against hers.

"Fiona," he says. "I have to ask you something. This isn't just a citizenship thing. When I'm with you, I feel like I'm going to make it, even though my plans have fallen to shit. You make me want to— well, *try*. I've stopped eating processed foods. I shut off the tap while I'm brushing my teeth. I gave up my seat on the train the other day— not to an old lady, either. To some bloke, just because he looked kind of tired. I really want to be the guy you deserve."

Fiona pulls her face away from his. She looks him in the eye.

"I want to ask you," he says, trailing off, emotion obstructing his windpipe. He swallows hard.

"Yes," Fiona says. "I know you love me, and you know I love you. Let's do it." She smiles, running her fingers through the Australian's thick, golden hair. "Let's get married."

As husband to Fiona, the Australian quickly gains a firm command of the nature of her dishonesty. He comes to realize that all of it is hope, simple as that. Hope for the ordinary and the slightly extraordinary, but never the extravagant. It embarrasses and infuriates him that her lies are simple and modest. He finds it alarming that some version of himself is housed in a mind so enchanted by the idea of a Checker cab sighting that it would manifest that enchantment in the form of a fib. Having lassoed his wife's greatest idiosyncrasy, the Australian gets down to the business of breaking it. She says: "I saw the prettiest thing today, an albino pigeon, but it still had those iridescent wings." He says: "Lie." She begins a story: "When I was a kid, I had this lunchbox—" and he cuts her off with: "Lie." Although this tactic deters her only slightly, the Australian vaguely senses that he is perpetrating something truly grotesque, and he is ashamed, which is not a feeling he is accustomed to. He begins to consider that he might have a deeper attachment to Fiona than he previously imagined possible.

Other strange things start to happen. Fiona's salary not only pays their rent but allows them to have a housekeeper, yet the Australian, who is unemployed, finds himself scrubbing and cleaning. He secretly fantasizes about enrolling in some kind of course, not a vocational one, but one that would provide him with a quiet means of self-expression. He wants to make something with his hands, be it a still life painting or a magazine rack or a savory soufflé. As the first year of marriage comes to a close, he begins to miss Fiona while she's gone from the apartment, off working on photo shoots and music video sets. The pop star is a notorious wreck and frequently depends on Fiona for support in times of crisis. She calls at all hours, hysterical on account of her boyfriend's addiction to Ginkgo biloba supplements, panicked over her incapability to trust herself around chocolate, distraught over the fast-approaching end of the Mayan calendar. The Australian has met her a handful of times and is certain she can't stand him, though Fiona says that is ridiculous. "Who wouldn't like you?" she says, laughing, but he cannot be dissuaded. Every time Fiona tends to her employer, the Australian feels sad and lonely and as though he's being robbed.

One night, when Fiona finally returns to bed after a two-hour phone call, he asks her to tell him a lie.

"You *want* me to lie now?" she asks.

"Yes," he pleads. "Just make something up for me."

"No." She sits up against her pillow. "It's your turn. Tell me a lie, something really outrageous."

"Okay," says the Australian. "I used to be a superhero."

It has been two years since the Day Club fiasco, and although the Australian makes money investing here and there, he has yet to find a new full-time job. He doesn't speculate on why his Wall Street ambitions faded or why Day Club fell through. Failure has integrated itself into the fabric of his being. Self-loathing is an intoxicating elixir—one to which, little by little, he has become habituated. By and large, he lives off Fiona's generous salary and the stipend she receives as part of the pop star's entourage. Fiona has decided to buy the apartment in which she and the Australian live, a two-bedroom in Chelsea with high ceilings and good light, but his anxiety about his own unemployment only mounts. Though the mortgage is in Fiona's name, he ought to contribute toward the payments, and he is embarrassed by his inability to do so.

Not to mention that he will be eligible to apply for a Green Card in about a year. The Australian fears his joblessness will be a hindrance.

"We're in a good position," Fiona assures him. "And you have some big opportunities coming up."

"No, I don't."

"Yes," says Fiona. "Of course you do." She is inviting him into one of her lies. "You have a lot brewing right now—like the interview for the position at the big, airy office with floor-to-ceiling windows and bowls of fresh fruit and mixed nuts, and a billiard table, too, where everyone will see how incredible you are."

"Right." The Australian forces a smile. "Of course."

"You'll see. It'll happen."

The truth is that on the occasions when the Australian has applied for a position and been granted an interview, he has botched it almost willfully, unable to stomach the idea of working under a boss. His days are spent doing intermediate-difficulty word puzzles in hotel lobbies, or wistfully watching construction workers on the job, or trying to learn Cantonese from an audio cassette, or wandering the streets.

One afternoon the Australian stumbles into a bookstore where an author is giving a reading. The author has a faded tattoo of a lizard on her bicep and is from Berkeley, California, and she has written a memoir from the perspective of her vagina. The Australian is transfixed. He stays for the whole performance, listening and watching from the back of the room, hiding behind a books-on-tape display at the edge of the children's section. He marvels at how, while every woman has a vagina, this particular woman has decided that hers deserved not only a voice, but a publisher, too, and maybe even a publicist. It is precisely the kind of boldness and ingenuity that the Australian respects. She barks out her vagina's litany of complaints, recounting its moments of triumph in a gurgling, throaty vibrato. Her vagina has adventures. It takes risks. The Australian is struck by the humbling realization that it might be more of a man than he presently is, this milksop he has become—drooling on his pillow, aimlessly wandering, pining for his wife—and he's got to buck up.

The Australian really likes Jim Foreman, whom he located in the back of *The New York Post*, because Jim is not a therapist, he would like to be very clear about that—he is a life coach. Jim is not a shoulder to cry on, and if the Australian is looking for soft tits to rub his face into, he is barking up the wrong tree. According to Jim, the Australian's problems derive from the fact he grew up fatherless, and the solution is to forge that connection and thereby discover his wolf spirit, but it is up to the Australian to figure out what that means for *him*. After his third session with Jim, the Australian is walking back to his apartment when he sees a window washer hanging from the side of an office building, and he is reminded of the only image of his father he has ever seen. It is a tattered, bleached-out photograph his mother had taken in the Gibson Desert during their weeklong fling, in which the Australian's father is abseiling down the side of one of the Kata Tjuta rock formations. The Australian remembers vividly how the fabric surrounding his father's groin was bunched into a formidable convexity by a leather harness, and how the tanned muscles of his bare calves looked like braided beef jerky.

He asks himself when he last faced his own mortality, but all he can come up with is the night a few months back when he choked on a bit of yellowtail sashimi. The incident occurred at a gala he had reluctantly attended with Fiona, at which the pop star had sung a cappella for the benefit of children with a certain dermatological condition. Although the description of the condition, which had been delivered with both levity and compassion by a well-known sitcom actor, had left the Australian rather nauseated, he had forged ahead to the buffet, only to get food down the wrong pipe. During those eternal seconds of complete tracheal obstruction, he really and truly feared for his life. The Australian is achingly aware that this incident is hardly comparable to mastering the steep, hot slopes of the Kata Tjutas, or freediving, or shark taunting, or BASE jumping, or any of the other things he's always imagined his father doing. He looks up again at the building, squinting against the sunlight, and as the window washer reaches far to his right, and the bench he is balancing on teeters just a little, the Australian finds his wolf spirit.

The moment in which the Australian considers that twenty-nine might be too old to take up parkour—the use of acrobatic maneuvers to overcome obstacles within an urban landscape, *l'art du déplacement*—is fleeting. Every time Fiona is out with the pop star, he does sit-ups and pushups while envisioning himself gracefully flipping over stairway banisters and leaping from building to building. When he announces his intentions to Fiona during a rare, shared dinner at home, she expresses skepticism and also genuine concern for his safety but ultimately supports her husband's desire to learn something new.

The Australian scours the Internet and identifies New York's top parkour instructor, a former internationally ranked traceur named Luc Chevalier. The first meeting takes place at a Central Park playground on a gray, drizzly morning in October. The Australian is relieved that the weather is dismal, because it means there will be fewer spectators for what he expects will be his first real attempt at athleticism in years—an event for which he has braved the chill in spandex bicycle shorts and an old T-shirt from his university days. When he arrives at the meeting place, Luc, whom the Australian instantly recognizes from the action shots on his website, is standing beneath a tree. He is dressed in black jeans and a red turtleneck, and is eating a Golden Delicious apple with great meticulousness. The Australian watches from an inconspicuous distance as Luc skims his teeth gently over the surface of the apple, virtually shaving it, and then savors each miniscule scraping for an impossible length of time. The Australian becomes mesmerized by the act and is quite startled when, without making eye contact, Luc finally swallows and says, "Do you know the meaning of the word *simulacrum*?"

Smiling and approaching the legendary traceur with his hand extended for a shake, the Australian concedes that he does not.

"This city is a simulacrum," says Luc, ignoring the Australian's hand and tossing his skinned apple into a nearby trash bin. "It is an artificial representation of an idea, a nightmare that we pretend is a memory—that we tell ourselves is a *reality*. A copy of a copy of a thing that never existed. Tell me something." He finally looks at the Australian. "Do you think this city should be here? Would you cry if it burned to the ground?"

The Australian isn't sure what is expected of him, but he nods vigorously.

"Of course you would," Luc continues. "You would cry, you would weep like a child whose ice cream fell into the sand on a hot summer day at the beach. That does not surprise me, not at all. Do you know *why* you would cry?"

"Because it would be a huge tragedy?" He senses he is in over his head. But although Luc terrifies him, he is eager for him to proceed.

"No," says Luc, staring off into the distance, where a swatch of city skyline rises up beyond the trees. "You would cry because you *believe* in this city—the buildings, the subways, this fence, that jungle gym. When you see a water fountain, you think, 'That is something I must walk *around*.' When you see a parking meter, you think, 'That is something I need to *avoid*.' Do you know what that makes you?"

"No," says the Australian, suddenly very self-conscious about his spandex shorts and considering the possibility that he is in the presence of genius.

"It makes you part of the simulacrum," says Luc. "That is what I'm here to fix."

Under Luc's direction, the Australian rapidly builds both physical and mental stamina, mastering the basic drop, the cat leap, the vault, and the gap jump over the course of just eight months. Upon surveying any landscape, his eyes automatically assess the most efficient, elegant way to travel from point A to point B, swiftly and creatively adapting to any obstacle in his path. He experiences his muscles first as ribbons, then as water, and eventually—once he really starts to achieve detachment from the simulacrum—as mere abstractions. Luc dictates that the Australian adhere to a strict meditation practice. Every morning the Australian wakes up at 4:45 a.m. and lies naked and with his eyes open for one hour, regardless of the weather, on the roof of the apartment building. As he lies there, he stares at the sky and envisions the gradual disintegration of the buildings, the cars, and the people, one molecule at a time.

During the initial stages of training, the Australian feels at *one* with Fiona and the city and himself, a fluidity of perception that gives him a pleasant sense of serenity. Then, as his stunt repertoire becomes more advanced and parkour becomes the lens through which he beholds all situations, he begins to pity people—first just some people, then most people, and finally all people. Fiona, whom the Australian once regarded as generous and hardworking, is revealed to be a petty and unstable woman, as evidenced by her inability to stand up to the pop star's demands on her time, and by several lapses in her proclaimed vegetarianism. A year into the mentorship, during a training session on the esplanade along the Hudson River, Luc confides that he's been anxious about some matters of personal finance. The Australian is struck with epiphanic

certainty that Luc is a poser, the worst kind of fraud: a so-called traceur who has yet to detach from the self. By the time the Australian
has mastered the double kong, the thief vault, and the under-bar
360, he is living in complete existential solitude, rapt in a state of
frantic and impenetrable bliss.

The Australian applies for a Green Card and is granted an interview.
At the immigration office, after a long wait in a crowded reception
area, an officer wearing a toupee at a perilously jaunty angle calls the
Australian and Fiona into a cubicle. The walls are aggressively beige
under the fluorescent lighting, and a philodendron sits wilting in a
corner. Fiona has lately expressed irritation at the Australian's continued unemployment and his attitude.

"It's like you think you're above everyone," she said. "I respect
your desire to experiment with a new perspective, truly. But maybe you're
looking through the wrong end of the binoculars."

Nonetheless, as she tells the immigration officer about the evening
they first met, their brief courtship, and their courthouse wedding, her
adoration is evident. When asked about her husband's professional
life, she states that although he has lately struggled to find work, she
believes in his potential.

"Elaborate, please," says the officer.

"Well," she says, "he can do anything. His mind is so sharp—
and he's creative, a very detail-oriented person. Wherever he ends up
working, he'll be amazing. He just needs to find the right fit."

The Australian answers questions about his employment history,
finances, and marriage. When asked Fiona's birthdate he fumbles,
and when prompted to describe the resources he is using for his job
search he says, simply, "The newspaper." The officer squints, as though

the Australian is a faraway bird whose species he can almost, but not quite, identify.

"And the Internet," the Australian adds. "Obviously."

In what seems to him an act of either saintly generosity or spectacular negligence, he passes the evaluation and is granted permanent residency.

The Australian now shuns most of his usual indulgences—television, pulpy fruit nectars over ice, lucid dreaming, taxicabs, heroic fantasies involving extreme weather events, caffeine, glossy magazines, crying, skin lotions, and socks—and yet he cannot seem to check his sexual impulses. Unable to abide Luc's hypocrisy, he quits parkour, deeming it nothing but trickery and show. Unchallenged physical fitness combined with spiritual euphoria increases his carnal appetites to proportions he finds difficult to reconcile with his otherwise ascetic existence. He repeatedly jerks off in the bathroom when all he ever intended was to brush his teeth. He is easily distracted by the sensuality of inanimate objects, such as peaches and clouds and bicycle seats. He becomes aroused at the slightest touch, the accidental caress of a cashier's finger brushing against his own leaving him restless and agitated for hours.

After several exhausting weeks of trying to remain diligent in his self-denial, the Australian unleashes himself on Fiona. She is by now very aggravated with him, sick of being judged and pitied and condescended to, but her punishment of him is symbolic. She too has finally developed frustrations of her own—working endless hours only to come home to a husband who has taken a weeklong vow of silence, or gone on a hunger strike. Her anger takes the form of nails scratching down the Australian's back, the biting of his neck, the too-tight gripping of her legs around his waist. The more estranged they become from each other, the more time they spend wrestling and tangling and bruising each other's bodies. Afterward, Fiona returns to the pop star and the Australian goes to the roof to meditate, until the aggravations of their separate lives reach their respective bursting points, and they collide once again in the middle.

As his parkour days slide further away, the Australian enters a period of profound psychic dissonance. While he aspires to holiness, coming so close during meditation as to bask in a tea-colored glow, at other times he is haunted by the realization that his instincts fall completely beyond the realm of his control. His consciousness is repeatedly assaulted by the notion that humans are, after all, just animals, and the thought causes numbness and tingling in his extremities. His mother was an early convert to the New Age movement, and at times fancied herself a reincarnated Aboriginal soothsayer. As such, she considered traditional Aboriginal proverbs a cornerstone of her parenting. While the Australian summarily rejected the proverbs as irritating symptoms of his mother's rather embarrassing affliction, and although he has had little contact with her since leaving Australia, he now finds himself taking solace in the poeticism of a particular proverb. In moments of acute disturbance—his discovery of a wiry hair growing from his ear, for example, or upon learning of Fiona's new friendship with a twenty-four-year-old hairdresser named Finn, who is, as it turns out, straight—the Australian says to himself, "Keep your eyes on the sun, and you will not see the shadows." When he feels rootless or forlorn, sorrowful or hungry—when he just wants his life to be normal, even to just know what normal *is*, to stop feeling like a handful of sawdust let loose in the wind—he repeats the proverb under his breath until it manifests as a vision.

In the vision, the Australian is in the middle of the ocean, on-board a pink and lime-green Jet Ski. The motor is broken. Sitting squarely upon the seat, he adjusts his center of gravity in accordance with the slow-rolling, deep-sea waves. He sees himself as if from the outside, a frail silhouette against a bright blue panorama. Upon that unlikely vessel, in the middle of a garish expanse, the Australian is nowhere; he is unknowable and beyond salvation. Reentering his body, he looks up, fixes his gaze upon the sun, and is instantly freed. As the glare overstimulates his cones and rods, all he sees is whiteness, followed soon after by the stripes and plaids and zigzags of impend-ing blindness. In that moment, within his own vision of himself, the Australian could be both anyone and anywhere.

In his day-to-day life, as he treads gingerly over the fragile surface of each passing hour, he wonders why he is so slippery that no plans or ideas can stick. He wonders at what point Fiona began to resent him, a likelihood suggested by her persistent avoidance of him despite the commencement of the pop star's yearlong hiatus. He wonders what happened to becoming rich and increasing muscle mass, to be-ing divine and transcending all the stuff—the needs and wants, things scooped out of him as if he were an overripe melon. He wonders what happened to his curiosity about the world, and to excitement, and to fashion sense, and to kindness. Again and again, he says to himself, "Keep your eyes on the sun, and you will not see the shadows." He says it whenever he needs to, wherever he may be.

"It'll blind you," Fiona says one night, when he whispers it like a prayer cast out to the center of their living room. It is a night they've spent together, churning inside the distended belly of their silence. "Staring at the sun will blind you," she says, clicking on the TV. "You know that, right?"

———

As winter falls upon the city, the Australian feels like a gray goshawk forced to live out the life of a domestic parakeet. He waits and waits for someone to forget to latch the cage, and meanwhile, unsure of how to pass the time, he pecks absentmindedly at whatever is in reach. Aside from the hour or two he spends in front of the computer analyzing the markets, his daily activities now resemble those of a nine-year-old on a day trip with his grandparents. He visits museums, goes window-shopping, walks in the park.

One day, the Australian goes to see a new exhibit on crystals at the Museum of Natural History. When he returns to the apartment, the first heavy snow of winter is falling outside the living room window, spinning the illusion of cleanliness around the city like fresh gauze. Fiona is sitting on the couch wearing a pair of the Australian's boxers and one of his old T-shirts, an uncharacteristic ensemble that both arouses and intimidates him. "Please sit," she says, curling her legs to make room for him on the couch. Her expression is peaceful, her posture oddly majestic. The Australian can tell she has been waiting for him all day, right there on that couch, and that something wild is about to happen. He sits slowly beside her.

"I don't know how it could've happened," Fiona says. "But I'm pregnant."

"Are you sure?" asks the Australian, who has witnessed her taking birth control pills every night of their marriage. For a split second, he wonders if the pregnancy might be a lie, but knows this isn't a lie she would ever tell.

"Six weeks," she says, smoothing hair away from her face.

There is no question, in the way she is speaking, of whether or not they will have a child—this the Australian understands.

"How is that possible?" he asks.

"It's a miracle." She cracks a smile. "A miracle baby, I guess."

While Fiona is only kidding, and the Australian knows this, the idea instantly electrifies him. He fights a series of urges—the urge to touch her stomach, the urge to ravage her, the urge to jump out the window—and instead configures his face into a reassuring smile. His expression is deliberately loose and peaceful and calming, and he's thinking about how, yes, in fact there has been loads of sex, but also that the pill should have prevented it, and it dawns on him that—between the incessant fornication and the unlikelihood of pregnancy—he is essentially a partial Saint Joseph.

While fatherhood has never held much interest for the Australian, pregnancy has been a lifelong fascination. When confronted as a child with his mother's nakedness, the idea that he had once been smothered and captive inside her doughy, freckled belly was simultaneously horrific and soothing. At fourteen, while traveling the New Zealand countryside with a friend and the friend's half-brother, he witnessed a baby lamb emerge from its mother encased in a slick, bloody sack, folded and rigid in a kind of suspended animation. The whole thing was startling in both its violence and its intimacy, like the sudden removal of a prosthetic nose, and images of it burst into the Australian's mind, seemingly without provocation, for years.

During times when he's felt like a force to be reckoned with, his fundamental inability to create life within himself has throbbed like an impacted molar. When lost in the fantasy of being pregnant, he has on occasion felt phantom fluttering in his lower abdomen and clenched his pelvic muscles as if in the grips of labor. While he is, on one level, quite embarrassed by all of this, he has decided to assume that all men share these feelings, thereby making a fuzzy kind of peace with them. He figures that pregnancy envy is yet another secret fact of manhood, just like feeling pleasantly infantilized in the barber's chair, or the desire to stumble upon and halt a brutal crime in progress.

It soon becomes plain that the Australian knows very little about the realities of pregnancy. During her first trimester, Fiona is tired and frequently vomits, not so much glowing as sallow and peeved. The Australian attempts to comfort her by reiterating that the conception was truly miraculous, at times going so far as to suggest that he himself is most responsible by virtue of his meditation practice. He cites a Swedish study demonstrating the ability of prayer to cause shape-shifting of the human body on the molecular level, but while this notion is very much supported by certain more progressive elements within the quantum physics community, Fiona seems not only skeptical but outright angry.

A long time ago, during a heated disagreement over the dignity of mustaches—Fiona was of the opinion that only certain, more conservative mustaches can be considered dignified, while the Australian's position staked its claim in the inherent dignity of *all* mustaches— Fiona had said, "Look, neither of us is going to bend. Would we rather be happy, or right?" While the Australian had been perplexed by the question, unable to comprehend why someone would forfeit his authority on any subject for any reason, he now begins to understand. He accepts that Fiona won't budge in her disbelief of miracles, nor will she give due credit to quantum physics, but he would rather be happy as husband and wife than continue his attempts to convince her, and so he lets it drop. What's more, whenever he wants to again invoke miracles, or to argue about some trivial matter, he now hears a queer, faint hum emanating from his yellow-gold wedding band, as though there were a mite-sized violinist balanced on the arc of it, playing whiny arpeggios in protest of the Australian's belligerent harping.

During those first unusually trying months, he brings Fiona tea and toast buttered on both sides. He looks at pictures of houses in architecture magazines with her, mostly large modern homes that appear to be plopped without much forethought into some seemingly random rural expanse, which she enjoys very much. He answers the phone when the pop star calls—now eight months into her hiatus—and takes messages for Fiona while she rests on the chaise longue, prostrate in the bluish winter daylight. By the time she begins to feel better, around her fourth month, it is apparent to both of them that the Australian is getting an unprecedented grip.

The Australian falls into a rhythm of extending himself to Fiona through acts of kindness and love. It is a stretching of himself that he finds pleasant and restorative, and because it is so deeply satisfying, he wants it more and more. Fiona's back begins to arch against the weight of the fetus, and the Australian, whenever he beholds her, is washed over by the desire to covet and protect. He offers to give her massages, run errands for her, do all the housework, but much to his bewilderment she resists. While she expresses her appreciation with sincerity, her inclination, since she is now feeling lively and energized, is to be active and self-sufficient. She begins working out at a Pilates gym using an apparatus called a "reformer," which strikes the Australian as a nouveau-medieval torture rack. She acquires several short-term jobs, including a personal shopping gig for an uptown debutante—a gaunt, doe-eyed heiress best known for her devotion to animal rights and her several petty theft convictions. The pop star remains abroad despite the fact that her career is fading in her absence, but Fiona is more active than ever. The Australian fears for the baby's health. Should she be exercising to the point of sweatiness and a flushed face? Should she be lifting large, boiling pots of water from the stove? Should she be walking everywhere in the summer heat? He has recurring dreams in which the baby is born prematurely, with skin as translucent as a Vietnamese spring roll.

Fiona assures the Australian that all is well, that she feels the fetus lively within her womb, kicking and hiccupping. She reminds him of the ultrasounds and examinations for which he was present, all yielding perfect results. Yet his anxiety persists. Fiona has planned to have her labor assisted by a doula, a lanky young woman named Fay, who is the daughter of a British human-rights documentary filmmaker. Fay, with her woven alpaca shoulderbag, a single dreadlock in her hair secured by a polished clove of nutmeg, has been coming to their apartment throughout the pregnancy. The Australian really likes her, and has noticed a significant expansion of his lung capacity in her presence. Since having a baby strikes him as a very serious matter, he appreciates that there is a professional in charge. Fiona, however, feels comfortable and assured in her body's capability and requires minimal assistance. This only heightens his sense that he is hooked to a slow-drip IV of espresso.

By the end of the pregnancy, the Australian is living in a whole new kind of love: an overamplified sanity, the clarity that just a few months ago had made his world so sharp and bright rendered shrill. It is too much now, which makes the Australian consider the possibility that he himself is too much—and after some thought he concludes it is true, but that regardless he will endure.

Early on a September morning, the Australian becomes a father. Fiona has decided to give birth at home, and so the first time he sees his son, he is a milky blur beneath the warm, pink water that halfway fills the inflatable birthing pool in which Fiona is reclined. As she pulls the baby up onto her chest, she says, "Oh," and in the mind of the Australian, who is kneeling in the living room beside her, that one syllable expands in infinite concentric circles around everything in the world that is good. He forgets about Fay, who is selecting the appropriate tool amongst the medical instruments spread out on a towel on the coffee table, and he forgets that there is a pigeon on the windowsill and honking horns below. He forgets what it is like to want something, the sight of the folded lamb, his misgivings about the human body.

A few minutes after the birth, Fay takes the baby, whom the Australian and Fiona have decided to call Maximus, and the Australian helps Fiona out of the pool. Fay does some things to Maximus, and the Australian helps Fiona into their bedroom and onto the bed, which is covered with towels and sheets, and then Fay does some things to Fiona. The Australian's eyes are fixed on his tiny son and his wife, Fay registering only as a sweet waft of patchouli. Then Fay is gone and the Australian is on the bed too, in the afternoon sunlight with his wife and baby, having forgotten about every other thing.

The high points of the Australian's marriage thus far have been rooted in mutual affection and shared sexual appetites, but rarely in deep understanding. In the days after Maximus is born, the Australian becomes aware of this. Expressions of adoration and awe and fatigue paint themselves across Fiona's face. She does things that she's never done before, sometimes with natural ease, other times with quiet frustration. Through one half-opened eye, the Australian beholds the stillness of her form as she nurses Maximus, awash in the oceanic light of an early morning. In this moment, Fiona seems ancient and unknowable. His wife has been this woman all along, but somehow he never noticed. Suddenly he wants not only to possess her, but also to comprehend her, yet he cannot summon the words to express this. He feels that to do so would be to break an unspoken yet irrefutable law dictating that all concerns outside of those directly related to Maximus are, from now on, to be abandoned. There are fundamental gaps in his marriage, crevasses of various depths, and efforts to bridge them must come from both him and Fiona. But there is no time. All of the time now is for Maximus, who in just a handful of weeks transforms from a pink infant, evocative of the plastic in-utero embryo at the obstetrician's office, to what appears to be a real baby.

For the first few months of Maximus's life, Fiona cares for him all day. The Australian is unaccustomed to her constant presence at home. It makes him feel awkward, unsure of what to do with himself. Not wanting his wife to witness his usual idling, he spends long hours at the computer shuffling around his meager investments. Now that, at long last, they are all three together, the needy and innocent presence of the baby keeps the Australian and Fiona separate, the enormousness of their creation wedged between them like a sky-high wall of blooming flowers.

Time passes, and the Australian, being a forgetful man—perhaps willfully so, although maybe at this juncture it is necessary—lets his realizations about the unfavorable state of his relationship with Fiona slide silently away.

Since the pop star has now finally returned to New York, it is agreed that the Australian will temporarily be a stay-at-home dad. Soon he will find a job with sufficient pay for a nanny to replace him as caretaker. When Maximus is four months old, Fiona goes back to work, and the Australian is left fully at the helm, eight hours a day. He has very little frame of reference for parenting, and as a result, his initial attempts are characterized by the spastic enthusiasm he associates with amateur interpretive dance. When Maximus cries, the Australian launches into a rigmarole: alternately smiling and grimacing for comedic effect, popping out from behind the couch or doorframe, babbling vowel-heavy nonsense, and singing medleys composed of the choruses of half-recalled New Wave dance hits. Fiona doesn't want Maximus to suck on a pacifier for fear he will develop buck teeth, so the Australian, concerned that his son is being denied some necessary comfort, spends hours a day sitting quiet and still with his soap-scrubbed finger pinched between the baby's gums. As he does, he naps or stares into space or reads the paper.

One day the Australian reads an article in the paper summarizing a study concluding that fatherhood leads to diminished testosterone levels, an evolutionary adaptation that allows once sex-crazed, brutish men to nurture and empathize. The Australian scoffs. A week later, while pushing Maximus in a carriage through a posh supermarket, he stumbles upon an unsettling scene. In front of a pyramid of pomegranates, and next to a glass-doored refrigerator containing several especially delicate varieties of orchid, crouches a man approximately the same age as the Australian. He is down by the side of his daughter, who is perhaps two years old, and he has produced from a large canvas bag what looks to the Australian like a bejeweled plastic throne. With horror, the Australian watches the man pull down his daughter's pants and underpants and seat her upon this throne. Unable to abandon a spectacle of this magnitude, the Australian looks on as the girl urinates, flanked by tables of produce. The man, oblivious to the milling crowds, praises her and chants, "Pee-pee, pee-pee,

pee-pee." The girl says, "All done," and the man then looks to the other shoppers with an expectant sort of pride.

Hurrying away, the Australian feels as though he has just witnessed an act whose devastation will alter humanity forever. He considers the event to be the sort of atrocity that could only happen in an upscale New York neighborhood, like dogs eating off the prix fixe menu, or the sale of two-hundred-dollar plastic bottles of water blessed by Tibetan monks via Skype. He tells himself that none of these things ever happen in Australia, and that, as he is and always will be an Australian at heart, he is therefore safe from such compulsions. But then he remembers the testosterone study, which emphasized the involuntary and unavoidable nature of the hormonal shift, and wonders if perhaps, in the name of paternal affection, violations of self and society are being committed all over the world. He imagines the plastic throne-potty in an Iranian mosque, the throne-potty under the strobe lights of a discotheque in Ibiza, the throne-potty in the middle of the Sahara Desert, the throne-potty faced toward a dazzling view of the Eiffel Tower. The Australian vows he will never be altered in such a way.

It is cold and drizzling on the walk home, and he fashions a rain shield for Maximus out of a sweatshirt. When they finally get to the apartment, Maximus is overtired, and once he is placed in his crib he begins to wail. The Australian, despite a headache and what has become a routine level of crushing exhaustion, sings the songs of his homeland, the songs of his childhood, until they both fall asleep.

The specific nature of Fiona's involvement with the pop star has always been something of a mystery to the Australian. He knows only the basics: that when the pop star goes on tour or shoots photographs or music videos, Fiona selects her belts and jewelry and scarves. He also knows that Fiona accompanies the pop star to major social events as well as more mundane engagements like doctors' appointments, salon visits, and the DMV. Now that he spends most of his time cooped up at home with Maximus, shouldering a responsibility whose gravity has been heretofore unfathomable to him, he often speculates on the lives of those in what he has come to think of as the outside world. He imagines the streets filled with well-rested adults half tipsy after sophisticated brunches, smoking cigarettes and cursing, all of them headed to the airport after being struck collectively by the whim to fly to Aruba.

The unknown aspects of Fiona's daily life become a matter of much speculation. While the Australian has avoided thinking about her work in the past, primarily because his own joblessness has been a source of shame, he now envisions her daily activities with obsessive intensity. What luxuries, he wonders, are currently being lavished upon her on the set of the latest music video? What cornucopia of delicious craft service snacks is splayed out before her, and does she often drink champagne with her lunch? Has she accompanied the pop star to work out a deal at the home of a record executive, and is this record executive European, and if so, does he have a name like Marc or Dmitri or Fernando? Does he have a hot tub in his living room, and does he smile knowingly? And what, the Australian asks himself one day, ever happened to Finn?

It is while watching daytime TV that Finn reinserts himself into the Australian's consciousness, right in the middle of a commercial advertising a contraption with which a woman might effortlessly style her hair into any one of several elegant configurations, including a French twist and a flawless chignon. The Australian first became aware of Finn on Fiona's thirty-second birthday—a mere year and a half ago,

although it now seems like another lifetime. She had chosen to celebrate it at a Russian tearoom during lunchtime on a Saturday, and
had persuaded the Australian to come along. Of the handful of Fiona's
friends in attendance, the Australian took special notice of Finn, whose
cheekiness and flamboyance reminded him very much of himself during his Superman days, and which therefore made him feel quite sad.

It was only when Fiona remarked several weeks later that Finn
had broken up with his girlfriend that the Australian became truly
anxious. It seemed that, from then on, every invitation from Fiona
that the Australian declined—an ear-candling appointment, for
example, or a fashion show by a designer who makes sexually pro-
vocative hospital gowns out of Japanese rice paper—was passed on to
Finn, who invariably accepted. It was humiliating for the Australian
to have his matrimonial slack picked up by this young dandy with
bleached highlights streaking the front of his golden hair. Yet the
Australian in no way confronted Fiona with his worries—those were
the days of rooftop meditation and transcendence and disregard for
worldly things—and eventually Finn seemed to fade, becoming just
another figure orbiting the pop star.

Now the Australian wonders if his perception of that fading is ac-
curate, or if he simply stopped listening. Perhaps nothing whatsoever is
going on, but at the very least an investigation will serve as a probe into
his wife's life at work. There is no mystery to diapers and spit-up and
naptime. All remaining mysteries in the household should therefore be
systematically eliminated. The Australian sets out to do that.

It is late afternoon when the Australian arrives via taxi at a cluster of
warehouses on the Brooklyn waterfront. Although it is May, there
is a chill in the air, and strong gusts rush off the river. He turns his

back to the wind in order to protect Maximus, who sleeps in a papoose strapped to the Australian's chest. Faded numbers are stenciled onto the sides of each of the three warehouses in peeling red paint, but Fiona's datebook didn't indicate in which warehouse the video would be shot. Just as the Australian reconciles himself to wandering the lot, the wind changes direction and the faint stutter of a drum machine reaches his ears. He follows the thumping sound until he finds himself at the entrance of the largest of the warehouses, a bare cement building the size of an airplane hangar. He tries a small side door. Finding it unlocked, he slowly opens it.

The harshness of white stage lights and the sudden cacophony wakes Maximus, but his cries cannot compete with the volume of the pop star, whose auto-tuned alto blasts into the gritty cavernous space through speakers lined up along one wall. The Australian stands unnoticed in the darkness, taking in the pop star's performance and the bustle of the crew. Fiona recently played the pop star's forthcoming album at home, so he recognizes the song—"Hot Heat." The pop star's career has suffered from age and her recent lack of output, and her performance for the video shoot strikes the Australian as an unsubtle declaration of hard times. Bound like a sprained ankle in white lingerie, she writhes upon the bare mattress of a canopy bed, lip-syncing the same few lines of the song take after take as two white men and one black man, all three of them shirtless in leather pants, stumble through their synchronized gyrations. Between takes, a tiny woman in black capris and a baseball cap coaches the dancers with evident frustration while the pop star gets her lips re-glossed.

Maximus stops whimpering and lets out a sigh, the warmth of which puffs against the Australian's neck. Between the fog machines and the stage lights, it is impossible for the Australian to see beyond the set, and he is unable to locate Fiona. As take follows take, the Australian grows bored, suspecting that he's seen all there is to see when suddenly, during a pause in the filming, Finn appears at the pop star's side with a canister of hairspray. His fingers move quickly around the perimeter of the pop star's face in a flurry of pinching and swooping, yet when he is done, her hair seems, to the Australian, entirely unchanged. Apparently satisfied, Finn disappears back into the darkness from which Fiona simultaneously emerges. She walks briskly across the warehouse toward the Australian, and for a moment he thinks he has been discovered. He dips out the side door, pulling it softly shut behind him. He stands in the damp chilly air for a few moments, anticipating a confrontation that never comes.

That night, Fiona returns home exhausted but eager as always to spend time with Maximus. She takes him into their bedroom. Nearly an hour passes, and when the Australian looks in on them, Fiona is sleeping in a chair while Maximus's drool pools warmly on her chest. The Australian gently takes Maximus from her and places him in his crib. When he returns, Fiona is in bed.

Although the Australian completed his mission undetected, he is by no means satisfied with his findings. As he lies in bed trying to sleep, he pictures Finn disappearing into the darkness and Fiona emerging from it, and he imagines what that darkness contains, and what people do there—what people *could* do there. He does not consider simply asking Fiona about her days or posing direct questions about Finn or any other aspect of her life. The Australian no longer considers direct conversation an option—maybe because adult exchanges between them have dwindled over the six months since Maximus was born, or maybe because questioning Fiona would expose the Australian's self-doubt. Above all, asking is less exciting than sneaking around.

When the Australian sets out the following day to a Tribeca spa known simply by its street address, 374, he feels wily, agile, like the desert dingo in one of his favorite childhood stories. It has lately occurred to him that there really is a piece of his father inside him, some twirling lasso of DNA that makes him restless and stupid and occasionally brave, but although fatherhood has spawned new curiosity in the Australian regarding his own origins, his father remains a lack he would rather not palpate. After locating the abandoned-looking building, the Australian stands across the street behind a tree, which shades a very alert Maximus from the summer sun while also hiding both of them from anyone passing through the entrance of 374.

Several minutes later, the Australian spots Fiona and the pop star, and he is oddly disappointed to observe that Finn is absent. The two women are laughing about something, and then Fiona touches the pop star's shoulder and gestures to her own teeth, prompting the pop star to aggressively and unabashedly pick from her own teeth some bit of food. Afterward, the pop star presents Fiona with an exaggerated smile, bearing all of her pearly veneers, and Fiona nods in approval. They turn their backs to the Australian and face the door. Fiona presses the tiny silver intercom button on a keypad embedded in the dirty brick. He sees her in profile mouth something that looks like "Seize us" or "Sea bug," perhaps some kind of code, but the distance makes lip-reading a challenge. When Fiona pulls open the heavy steel door, the Australian sees that there is no lobby, just a short cement-floored hallway lit by a naked bulb that terminates in a dangerous-looking freight elevator. Then the door closes and the two women are gone.

A few minutes later, after determining that there is no video surveillance at the building's entrance, the Australian saunters up to the door, tells Maximus to hush, and presses the buzzer. He is surprised by the coolness of the little silver button, and is distracted by the unexpected tactile sensation to such an extent that when the intercom clicks on he is taken aback. Refocused, he waits for a voice to come through, but none does, and he doesn't know what to say. The rushing sound of the intercom shuts off. Again he gathers himself and presses the button, and again the rushing sound is unbroken by a human voice. By now the Australian is very nervous. He blurts out, "Seize us," and then quickly turns, carrying Maximus the eighteen blocks home.

Over the next few days, the Australian's obsession with Fiona's activities intensifies. He lives half in the world and half in jealous fantasies of his wife having an affair with Finn—and perhaps many other men. He begins tailing Fiona. He peers through the windows of the Pose Posse women's yoga studio, where Fiona sits flipping through a glossy copy of *Indonesian Vogue* while the pop star, having vanished into some brightly lit back studio, is presumably contorting her body into the very same postures she once demonstrated in an infamous pornographic flip book. The flip book had first been published nearly a decade ago, and as the Australian watches Fiona slowly turn magazine pages, he is surprised by his own dull yet undeniable sense of dread as he reflects upon the fact that the pop star is now fifty.

The next day he watches from behind a parked florist's van as Fiona escorts the pop star into a futuristic hat shop called Haberdasher F, a converted West Village brownstone from which the women emerge after two long hours with nothing. So the days go by, with a break for the weekend, during which the Australian cooks a dinner of rosemary chicken and then makes love to Fiona in a rigid missionary position.

The Australian begins to lose interest in Finn, who has not made an appearance since the video shoot. Maximus is a mild-tempered baby, not prone to fussing, but he soon tires of spending his naptimes upright in the papoose, and managing him during the excursions becomes increasingly difficult.

Finally, the Australian himself grows weary of the quest, but it is precisely on the day he decides to quit that Fiona mentions Finn. She invokes his name in the context of an upcoming award show at which the pop star will be performing a ballad off the new album, called "I Can't Free Me (from Myself)," and instantly the Australian is back to snooping.

"What's that, then?" he asks, his forced casual tone registering frightfully nasal and snappish to his own ears.

"Finn and I have to get together to plan her palette—her *look*," she says. "So I'll be home late tomorrow."

"No worries." He nearly scalds his hands and forearms as he pours a pot of hot pasta water too quickly into the sink. "Do your thing, love. I'll be home with Maximus."

The next evening, the Australian arrives half an hour early at Ceremony, the Japanese teahouse where the meeting is scheduled. Clearly unaccustomed to the presence of babies, the maître d' looks quizzically at Maximus, who has just awoken after being lulled by the taxicab ride and now blinks at his surroundings. The maître d' glances at the Australian as if to say, *Are you sure?* The Australian nods and follows the host to a semi-private cubby near the back, a dimly lit nook enclosed on three sides by semi-translucent paper walls decorated with pressed, dried flowers. He sits down at the very low stone-slab table upon a black satin cushion, lifts Maximus from the papoose, and plops him into his lap. When a waitress comes to take the Australian's order, he is so frantically attempting to distract Maximus, whose bedtime is now imminent and whose lower lip has begun to tremble, that he brushes off her quiet "What can I get for you?" with "Whatever you'd recommend." Ten minutes later the Australian is drinking an eighty-five-dollar pot of tea.

Fifteen minutes later, he hears the bell-like sound of Fiona's voice conversing with a man's voice that must belong to Finn, perhaps two cubbies away.

"How about a festive palette? Mardi Gras, maybe," says Fiona.

"I'm not sure if that's enough for this gig," says Finn. "I think we should do some kind of fusion." He is excited and suddenly quite loud. "Like, synthesized as fuck. Blow their minds."

"Flapper meets hippie?" suggests Fiona, not sounding nearly as excited as Finn. "Those can mesh nicely."

While Maximus seems to have intuited the need for silence, the Australian feels something welling up inside of himself, something terribly alive.

"No," says Finn. "I'm talking animal skins meets *Little House on the Prairie*."

"Oh," says Fiona, sounding tired.

"I'm talking Queen Elizabeth meets Van Gogh in the gutter." Finn is nearly shouting. The Australian holds his breath. "Red-light district meets—I'm just thinking out loud here. Midwestern beauty pageant contestant meets turn-of-the-century Ellis Island immigrant."

To the Australian's horror, laughter explodes from him, the brute force of which strains his stomach muscles as he tries to contain it. Maximus begins to cry, a piercing shriek, and in a matter of seconds Fiona is standing at the opening of the Australian's cubicle.

During his twelve years in New York, the Australian has found friendships difficult to sustain. He's made various connections here and there, but they've all been based upon his fleeting passions. There had been Wall Street acquaintances, coke buddies, parkour companions, but upon the termination of each involvement, the associated friendships quickly dissolved. He feels a great nostalgia for his youth in Australia, where according to his memory he was never alone. In university, he had seemingly dozens of best mates, all of them equally attractive and quick-witted, with an uncomplicated enthusiasm for having fun. He remembers the rough physical affection he shared with those friends—shoves and gut punches and high fives—and the merciless pranking, their unapologetic love of meat, and the ease with which they carried on conversations about dreams and sex and surfing. Be it a matter of age or culture, the Australian has never been able to identify his comrades among the black-clothed, frail-looking men of the hip, downtown New York scene in which he haphazardly became entrenched.

It is while Fiona is standing at the opening of his cubicle at Ceremony, looking down at him where he sits on the ground holding Maximus, that he looks beyond his wife's mystified and then angry face to Finn who stands behind her, and in that instant—despite the fractal of embarrassment presently expanding from his solar plexus—realizes he has finally found a friend.

As the Australian humiliates himself by providing Fiona with honest answers to her questions about what he is doing at the teahouse and how long he has been following her, he discovers Finn's expression is neither pitying nor condemning. On the contrary, he wears a faint smile that suggests he considers himself in on a clever joke, one he approves of wholeheartedly. When the Australian confesses to Fiona that Finn is the object of his suspicion, and when Fiona, in response to the admission, asks the Australian if he has lost his mind, Finn's expression changes to one of admiration. Fiona admonishes the Australian for his dishonesty and distrust of her, things she feels she doesn't deserve, and also for dragging Maximus along past his bedtime. The Australian listens and feels very remorseful, but then Finn—who has been handed the checks for all their teas by the waitress in an effort to get them to leave the restaurant—steps in.

"Fiona," he says. "What I see is a man who loves his wife so much that it's driven him a little crazy. But isn't that every woman's dream?" He goes on to lay out the parallels between madness and love, explaining how insanity is the purest form of romance.

"What the hell are you talking about?" says Fiona.

"She's right," says the Australian. "I was wrong to do this."

"You *were* wrong," says Fiona. She takes Maximus from the Australian and storms out of Ceremony.

The two men are left alone.

"Thanks for your help, pal," says the Australian, shaking Finn's hand.

Finn looks into the Australian's eyes, then toward the door through which Fiona has just exited. "Damn," he says, shaking his head. "That's love, man."

At home, the Australian apologizes again. He does his best to take responsibility and not make excuses, but the very sound of his voice seems to disgust her. When he places a hand on her shoulder, she jerks away.

"I don't want to look at you right now," she says.

"Because I was foolish?" asks the Australian. "Because I did a stupid thing? I admit it, I made a mess of things."

Fiona sits down on the end of their bed and closes her eyes.

"You always make a mess of things," she says, as if to no one, or to herself.

"That's not true. What do you mean?"

"There are so many opportunities out there for a guy like you. I work my ass off, and you still have no job. How is that possible? You could do anything." She grabs his hand and flips it so his palm is facing up. Then she squeezes his hand into a fist and drops it. "It's like everything falls through your fingers."

"We're still together," says the Australian. "I'm sticking with you." It occurs to him at precisely that moment that he can't remember the last time Fiona told a lie. The realization is like a burn, a lack of sensation followed by a mounting ache. "I'm sticking with you," he repeats, waiting for affirmation from her, some kind of acceptance or appreciation of his promise, but none comes.

The next day Fiona is distant, her interactions with the Australian stiff and deliberately cordial. A week later, nothing has changed. The Australian realizes Fiona's anger must have been building for a long time. Months ago she told him, "I feel like I show my whole self to you, and you aren't paying attention. You just can't seem to see beyond yourself. You can't step into my reality, or you won't—not even for half a second." Her remarks had stung, and now they return to the Australian often.

He dimly suspects that Fiona's anger is justified. Still, surely by this time he has made penance for the spying episode, and the extended punishment is uncalled for. He begins to return Fiona's coldness with a dismissive attitude of his own. Furthermore, he can think of no reason he should not contact Finn, whom he'd taken a fancy to during their brief exchange at the teahouse, and ask him out for a drink.

———

The Australian sits waiting for Finn in a Greenwich Village bar called Señor Sparky's. It is located on a lively street, tossed in amongst comedy clubs, falafel joints, tattoo parlors, and coffee shops, two blocks away from Washington Square Park and the NYU campus. The Australian is a connoisseur of daiquiris and finds those at Sparky's—made with the winning combination of fresh strawberries and shitty tequila—to be superior. The bartender, a pockmarked German named C.J., habitually gives free drinks to the old-man chess players from the park, an exchange the Australian loves to witness, although it would be hard for him to articulate exactly why. He has been to the bar on a handful of occasions, but always at odd hours and not since Maximus was born, and only now that it is primetime happy hour does the bar's vicinity to the university become meaningful. Three shiny-haired girls, two of them in tube tops, sing karaoke in front of a large flatscreen TV across whose screen march the lyrics to an eighties power ballad. Undergraduate students crowd on barstools around frothy beer pitchers resting atop high tables, and a few graduate students sit drinking alone or in pairs at the bar, one with a laptop, a few others with books.

The bar is so loud that when the Australian spots Finn, looking out of place in black leather pants and a red, Western-style button-down shirt, the Australian has to call his name three times before Finn catches his eye. The Australian immediately recognizes sorrow in the way Finn's eyes and mouth droop downward and the painful smile that is more of a tense pursing of the lips. After the men greet each other, they agree upon a pitcher of strawberry daiquiris. Drinks in hand, the Australian asks Finn what is the matter.

"It's my girlfriend," says Finn. "Vivian. She's left me."

The Australian—feeling he can relate more than Finn might imagine, given the iciness of his relations with Fiona, but not wanting to say so quite yet—puts his hand on Finn's shoulder in solidarity. "Sorry, mate," he says. "What happened?"

"Well, this isn't the first time," says Finn.

"If she came back the other time, maybe she'll be back this time."

"That's the thing." Finn closes his eyes, takes a deep breath, then looks down at his drink. "It didn't happen just one other time. It's happened many times. It happens every few months."

"Sounds like you'd be better off without her, then," says the Australian. "If she can't stick with it, stop riding the roller coaster." He recalls Fiona's condemning of him, her assertion that he can't stick with anything, and feels indignant. "Find someone who appreciates you," he adds.

"Oh, but she does." Finn looks up from his drink and into the Australian's eyes. "She loves me more than anything. It's just that she can't help it."

"She can't help what?"

"Vivian is polyamorous." Finn's tone is one of exhaustion and defeat. "And when she's seeing a new person, she tells me about it, every last gory detail. She says that honesty is crucial to a healthy poly relationship, but I get so upset. Then she decides we need time apart, and I don't see her for weeks. There's nothing she can do about her, you know, tendency. She says it's the way she was born."

"She was *born* polyamorous?" The Australian simultaneously feels compassion for his new friend and also relief at the state of his own union with Fiona. Whatever is going on in Finn's relationship seems far more difficult than anything he and Fiona have faced. "Can't she change for you?"

"It's probably genetic," says Finn. "That's what she says, anyway. In terms of evolution, it makes sense. Competing sperm and all that."

"I say lose her. Find a girl who only wants to be with you."

Finn pours more daiquiris into both their glasses, pulls an electronic cigarette out of his breast pocket, and explains that he's quitting smoking. "Don't know what's harder to quit," he says. "Vivian or cigarettes."

The karaoke girls are now singing one of the pop star's early singles, the up-tempo title song off her first album, *Hey!*

"I hear you," says the Australian. "Love can be brutal." Revealing his marital problems seems an awkward prospect considering Finn's friendship with Fiona. The Australian wonders what, if anything, she has told him.

The next morning, the Australian is cleaning up after breakfast. It is the first warm day of spring and Fiona is at work. The kitchen is an open space from which the Australian can safely keep an eye on Maximus, who is gnawing on a teething ring while sitting on a blanket in the living room. The Australian bends over to turn on the dishwasher, and when he looks back toward the living room, Maximus is no longer at its center. Approaching the vacated blanket, the Australian sees that his son has crawled over to the couch and hoisted himself up to stand. It is the first time he has done this, and he appears to the Australian like a bewildered conquistador, stunned by his newfound power.

From some subterranean region of the Australian's brain comes a powerful conviction that Maximus must see Australia. Whereas he had never given the role of heritage much thought before in relation to his son's upbringing, it strikes the Australian as vital in this moment that his son love, and feel loved by, his homeland. He wants to take Maximus to the Outback and tell him, as a childhood friend of his once did, that "kangaroo" means "I don't know what you're saying" in the language of certain Aborigines. He wants Maximus to know his grandmother—the Australian's mother, Margaret, whom the Australian has spoken to only once since Maximus's birth, but who has sent several letters imploring him to visit and bring his family. He wants Maximus to eat at his favorite restaurant in Melbourne, a Greek joint called Stalactites, and to surf at the beaches of Sydney and to sift through the sand for shark's teeth, just as the Australian did in his youth.

In the beginning of his relationship with Fiona, she had expressed keen interest in visiting Australia, but at the time he had been reluctant, on account of his embarrassment at returning home without much to show for himself in the way of a career. Later, as Fiona's commitment to the pop star deepened, such an excursion became impractical.

Maximus teeters back on his heels and then falls onto his bottom. The Australian offers him a single finger by which to pull himself up, but Maximus is no longer interested in the adventure. The Australian decides that as soon as Maximus is no longer a baby—when he is perhaps six years old—he will take him on a voyage to the Lucky Country.

Over the following weeks, the Australian and Finn unite like brothers, but with the speed and intensity of first love. Fiona has always encouraged the Australian to become more social. But although she doesn't say so outright, it is clear that his near-constant companionship with one of her coworkers, one of her own friends, was not what she had in mind. He deems his wife's perturbation insignificant compared to the benefits of his new friendship, and so he surrenders without a second thought to her quiet disapproval.

The Australian has always thought of New York City as an achingly lonely place, the length of Manhattan like an arm extending toward something forever out of reach, the boroughs a collection of nets catching stray souls drifting out to sea. Only now that he has found a kindred spirit in Finn does it occur to him that he has been a profoundly lonely person—that his alienation was not the city's fault so much as the circumstances of his life there.

The Australian realizes that he has been profoundly sad all along. That although he loves Fiona, she has never been completely and entirely his, and that although his heart wells with tenderness and adoration at the thought of Maximus, a man needs more company than that of a baby. The laughter and activities the Australian now partakes of with Finn seem to be curing the soul sickness that had made him feel the dejection and hunger of a street urchin on some wintry night, staring longingly through a window into some impenetrable, warmly lit domestic heaven. Now, walking down the streets with Finn, the buildings no longer seem to sway with sorrow, nor do the clucks and coos of pigeons register as heckling. The Australian has always perceived the crowded avenues of the city as vampiric, violently penetrating the membrane that contains him, guzzling his life force. These days he submits himself freely to the centers of the bustling throngs, contentedly submerged in the rivers of pedestrians, finding sustenance and inspiration in motion and sweat and the mysteries of strangers' lives.

The Australian's shame begins to dissipate. Suddenly lighthearted about his many aborted ventures, he takes Finn to witness an elite parkour demonstration put on by some old acquaintances. Finn, in turn, arranges for the Australian to accompany him to an international Ping Pong competition. The Australian brings Finn to his favorite crêperie in the East Village, and Finn takes the Australian to a hand-pulled noodle shop in Chinatown. They exchange secrets—jealousies, regrets, and fantasies—unburdening themselves to such an extent that, at the end of more than one conversation, both men agree that they feel lighter, slimmer, younger. Looking back across the wide plains of his newfound freedom, the Australian recalls the desperate quest for his wolf spirit, a mission that seemed so harrowing. He knows now that the quest was futile. It is not a matter of seeking out your wolf spirit, he now believes, but of waiting patiently until your wolf spirit comes to find you.

Six weeks after Finn's breakup with Vivian, the inevitable reuniting occurs. The Australian immediately takes a liking to her. Whereas he had previously envisioned a femme fatale, a leather-clad vixen with lips painted the most sinister shade of red, Vivian is in fact amiable and bookish, but without any hint of pretension. She reminds him very much of studious and fresh-faced Dolly, a neighborhood girl in Melbourne whom he was fond of as a boy. Vivian is quite serious about certain subjects such as national politics, feminism, and the media's fetishization of artists' eccentricities solely for the purpose of satisfying the general public's preconceived notions about artists. Vivian herself is an artist, having recently enrolled in film school, yet she is openhearted and easy to be around.

The first time Finn brings Vivian along for an excursion with the Australian, a mid-week lunch in the back garden of a tiny pasta shop in Little Italy, she captivates the Australian with stories about the Annual Starship Symposium, a conference in Orlando, Florida, that she and Finn had attended the previous year. Most of the scientists at the

symposium were affiliated with agencies like NASA and DARPA—
one of them, a nuclear physicist from Stanford, was a distant relation
of hers—and were there to present cutting-edge information about
interstellar space travel. She describes huge lecture halls teeming with
men and women wearing too-short khakis and pocket protectors,
wild-eyed in their collective ambition to venture into deep space,
buzzing with hunger for the awesome freedom of finally leaving the
Milky Way behind. It was there that she shot the short documentary
that earned her acceptance to film school.

Vivian's descriptions command the Australian's daydreams for
weeks. He thinks about all of those scientists vibrating with the hope
that having come together they might somehow reorganize all of their
disparate beliefs, laboratory findings, and the conventions of their areas of study in such a way that a unified dream will be made manifest.

The duo becomes a trio—a quartet, counting Maximus—and
the Australian, on one golden summer afternoon as they picnic beside the fountain in Washington Square Park, realizes that for the
first time since he emigrated over a decade ago, he feels at home in
this spectacular metropolis.

PART TWO

THE AUSTRALIAN KNOWS HIS father only from stories told by his mother, Margaret, about the few short days of their acquaintance. However improbable, the stories support everything he wants to believe about his father, and so he has always accepted them as fact. At twenty-three years old, Margaret was a well-mannered young woman looking to reinvent herself—to break away from her stern, mustachioed father, half-pickled mother, and the trappings and obligations of coming from a prominent Melbourne family. She decided to hitchhike to Alice Springs, where she planned to meet a friend she knew from her days at an all-girls' boarding school. The two young women intended to spend a few months at a naturalist campground smoking marijuana and making crafts.

The Australian's father made his fateful entrance during a pit stop along the way: a dank, smoky bar in rural Victoria, on the border of New South Wales. As Margaret stood alone ordering a beer from a toothless barmaid, the musky-smelling stranger beside her touched her shoulder. Smiling devilishly, he offered to buy her drink. He introduced himself as Lock Jones, and upon inquiry revealed that Lock was short for Lochlan and that he was a direct descendant of a clan of Scots born of Norwegian Viking settlers. "But don't ask me about the Loch Ness Monster," he said. "It's all cock and bull." His great-grandfather had immigrated to Australia during the first gold rush, following the legendary prospector Edward Hargraves and his enterprising legions to Bathurst, New South Wales in 1851.

Lock's forehead was high, with a protruding ridge of bone along his sun-leathered brow, his teeth straight and luminous with prominent canines, hands thickened by calluses. He wore tight, scandalously abbreviated denim cut-off shorts and a sun-bleached, olive-green short-sleeved shirt, which at first led Margaret to surmise that he worked maintenance or lawn care at a nearby golf resort. But when she asked what he did for work, he laughed and proclaimed that work was for fools.

"Leave the jobs to the drongos, missy," he said. "I'm an adventurer."

"An adventurer?" said Margaret. She had begun to feel antsy, her flesh tightening against her bones as if she were in the presence of a snake. She drank her beer quickly, intending to get back on the road. Lock appeared to deliberately withhold his response, and she rolled her eyes. Knocking back the last swig, she slung her leather satchel over her shoulder. It was precisely at this point in the telling of the story that, on the many occasions she related it to the Australian, she always began to fan herself with her hand.

"An adventurer," Lock finally said, leaning in toward her and lowering his voice conspiratorially, "is a bloke who isn't going to let a girl as gorgeous as you leave this bar alone."

Margaret froze as her eyes met his. His irises were the same fresh green as an aloe leaf. The thick plume of a nearby patron's pipe smoke clouded the space between their faces, then loosened into wispy tendrils that were sucked away by a lazy ceiling fan. The tension was almost unbearable, but Margaret suddenly felt that relief lay not in retreating but in fulfilling the moment, whatever that might mean. She thought of her parents lobbing weak, underhanded serves on their private tennis court, and of the gals she'd grown up with marrying off, squeezing out babies, striding with mindless enthusiasm toward decrepitude.

Without breaking eye contact, Lock pressed upon her shoulder until she sat back down on her barstool. In place of the fear that perhaps she ought to have felt at the aggression of this rugged stranger's advances, she was possessed by the desire to overpower him. The desire came from the part of her that felt inexplicably and suddenly magnetized by this man, but didn't want to be taken this way—plucked like a plum dangling conveniently from some low bough.

"Maybe it's you who will be leaving with me," she said. "Not the other way around."

"Oh yeah?" said Lock, raising his brow.

"Maybe it's *me*," she continued, "who wants to take *you* on a real adventure."

If every moment in this life is a challenge—Margaret always said this to the Australian at the end of the story—and if in any given moment there is a winner, then she, there in that bar, was victorious.

The other story about Lock Jones that Margaret often told was the tale of the Australian's conception. He was eight years old when she first chose to acquaint him with the particulars of the event, which had occurred on the night after she'd taken Lock's photograph as he scaled and then abseiled down the steep, red rock face of the Olgas in Uluru-Kata Tjuta National Park. Having spent nine months in the Outback as apprentice to a Turuwal Aboriginal boomerang-maker, Lock professed to know the terrain, climate, and wildlife as well as any white man ever could. He spoke knowingly about the telltale signs that the roots of a particular eucalyptus tree were home to mature witchetty grubs, the giant larvae of several moth species whose lightly charred bodies, he promised, tasted as sweet and summery as fresh corn. With vivid exactness, he described the process of capturing and preparing *Tjati*—small, red lizards that had provided vital sustenance to the Aborigines for millennia.

It was under the pretense that Lock was a practiced survivalist and capable desert guide that Margaret breathlessly telephoned her friend in Alice Springs to explain that her arrival would be delayed indefinitely, and agreed to venture into the Gibson Desert on foot with a man she'd known for three days—one of which had been spent in the hot leather passenger seat of his battered pickup truck, the other two shacked up in a blooming flower-wallpapered room at Camellia Court Motor Lodge.

After driving past Ayers Rock and on through the seemingly infinite and arid expanse, Lock and Margaret parked the truck in the visitors' lot near the Olgas—rounded, rust-colored rock formations like red bubbles rising from the dusty desert floor. Wide-eyed and heart aflutter, Margaret watched as Lock climbed the smooth, dizzying incline, barefoot and carrying an old camouflaged rucksack, a memento from his brief stint in the Royal Australian Air Force several years earlier. When he reached the top of the gargantuan boulder, he stood grinning down at her and the two dozen tourists who had gathered to witness and photograph his ascent under the yellow sun.

Margaret marveled at the brilliance of Lock's teeth, which, even at that distance, were positively phosphorescent. He removed from the rucksack some rope, a harness, and something small and shiny and metal—a clip, it soon became clear—and rigged himself up in preparation for his descent. It proved to be a swift and wild display of fearlessness and agility. Without shifting her gaze away from Lock's acrobatic form, Margaret withdrew her camera from her satchel—a brand-new Bantam Colorsnap, of which she was very proud. She raised it to her heart-shaped face and peered through the viewfinder. As Lock came into focus, magnified by the powerful zoom, she suddenly had a premonition that he was either not long for her world, or not long for this world, or both. In that instant she dreaded the stillness with which he would be captured in the resulting photograph, but knew with that prescient and total sort of knowledge that seems to burst through from some other place that the moment would one day be a memorial to something greater than the lust and thrills she and Lock would share.

She did not yet know that, later that same day, Lock would lead her trekking deep into the Outback until bats flitted through the purple dusk and kangaroos dotted the horizon, and it would gradually become apparent, despite his vehement denials, that they had lost their way. She didn't yet know that he would have forgotten the old army blanket in the bed of the pickup, not until both of them were exhausted and the night air had thinned and chilled, or that they would quarrel about their predicament until the yowls and yips of dingoes stirred fear in her, fear she was too proud to admit, and which caused her to consume Lock with her body like a sweaty fist clenching a hot coin.

All that night she would wring perspiration and sperm from him until he appeared to have physically diminished, withered into a frail husk, and she was too tired to stay awake, finally slipping into a twitchy sort of half sleep, all the while vowing that she would leave this wanker in the morning. She didn't know that, by morning, two vital cells—one his, one hers—would be united. A month after that, the Australian would be a firm, tiny cluster of tissue, and a few months later he would wake Margaret in the night with his kicks and hiccups, and a few months after that, after only two and a half hours of labor, he would be born—red-faced, green-eyed, insatiable.

All of these things had yet to occur. But as she watched through the camera's cross-hatched viewfinder, the distance between her and Lock Jones shrinking as he made his descent, and as she admired the defined musculature of his tanned legs, the radiance of his smile, his impossible bravery—and in the instant the shutter clacked—she sensed that the photograph would one day have significance beyond anything she could foresee. "It was as if I knew you'd be coming," she would tell the Australian throughout his boyhood. "Somehow I knew it before you'd even begun."

Aside from these two stories, the Australian's mother only ever provided him with occasional snatches of information about Lock Jones. These spontaneous recollections punctuated the Australian's early years, torturing him with their vagueness, their merciless brevity. They were provoked at times by something readily apparent: a fishmonger at the outdoor market with Lock's jaw, fanned out like the wings of an old Cadillac; the various failures and shortcomings of Margaret's ceaseless parade of beaus, which often inspired her to wistful recollection; an illustration in the Australian's secondary school physics textbook depicting the mechanism by which a boomerang makes its return.

On other occasions, when Margaret spoke of Lock, the Australian could perceive no obvious trigger. There was the time she took the Australian on a train journey up through Queensland to visit some distant cousins, and she exclaimed in her sleep: "Lock! Haven't you been listening to a bloody word I've said?" While snipping the Australian's seashell-pink toenails with little scissors, she once paused to say, "It only took me two hours with your father to discover that he had poor eyesight, but God save the soul who tried to convince him to buy a damn pair of glasses." And on a warm Christmas morning, as she and the Australian lay on the two old couches in their living room, stuffed to the ears with plum pudding: "Your father never mentioned having gone to school or reading books, nothing along those lines. I'm quite sure he was illiterate. Still, he spoke like a man who'd read all the classics."

At the seaside town of Geelong, where Margaret's parents had a beach house to which she had taken the Australian during his summer holidays, she once spoke of Lock Jones at uncharacteristic length while helping the Australian build an enormous sandcastle.

"One time, I saw your father cry," she said, smoothing the seaward wall of the precarious structure with the palm of her hand. "He was driving the truck, and I'd fallen asleep in the passenger's seat. I woke up because we'd stopped moving. I opened my eyes to see that we'd parked by the side of the road in the middle of the desert. The sun was going down. It looked like the horizon was melting, the way it rippled in the heat. We were on our way to Alice Springs, where I'd asked him to leave me. I looked over at him, wondering why he'd stopped driving, and I saw that he was crying. His tears were tiny, like itty-bitty specks of glitter on his cheeks. I'd never seen tears so small."

"Why was he sad, Mum?" the Australian asked, putting down his shovel.

"Oh," said Margaret, dripping wet sand through her fingers to create a spire on a fragile tower. "I'd like to think it was because he knew I'd be gone soon. But maybe it was just the sunset."

At eleven years old, the Australian crept into his mother's bedroom, stealthy as a robber, although he was home alone. He rifled through her sewing basket and underwear drawer, through shoeboxes filled with tarot cards, through the wicker bin containing her crystal collection and then both of her jewelry boxes in search of the picture of Lock Jones abseiling down one of the Olgas. He had seen his mother bring it out from her bedroom several times but didn't know precisely where she kept it. She had a chest in which she kept private possessions, and the Australian feared the photo might be in there, sequestered by lock and key.

Finally he found it tucked between the pages of his baby book, which she kept lodged on a high closet shelf. The snapshot had been slipped between a page onto which a silky tuft of the Australian's hair was taped—*Baby's First Haircut*, Margaret had written underneath—and a page exhibiting a grocery receipt decorated with the infant Australian's scribblings. Careful not to smudge the old photograph's lingering sheen, the Australian took it to his bedroom, where, after studying it for several heartbreaking minutes, he hid it beneath his mattress.

Over the following years he often examined the picture for signs and codes, for clues as to his father's whereabouts, for some indication of whether or not his father knew he had a son. The Australian watched the picture for changes, as if one of his father's sun-gold hands might somehow magically penetrate the walls of the apartment, his bedroom, the heft of his mattress, the obstinate laws of space and time, and alter the image in order to affirm him in his tenuous belief that he was not, and had never truly been, alone—that he was not really a bastard son. Throughout the Australian's adolescence, and then during his years at university, he treasured the picture, stowing it away in secret, for his eyes only. Although Margaret must have been aware of its disappearance, she never let on. She had always been unreceptive to the Australian's questions about his father, dismissing them with a sad smile before changing the subject. The Australian could only assume that her reasons for avoiding those discussions were the same reasons she didn't confront him about the missing snapshot.

At twenty-two, he brought the picture with him to New York City, hiding it in a manila envelope in the back of the dresser drawer in which he kept his socks. For years it remained there, fading, its edges curling, its white border yellowing. He never showed it to anyone, not even to Fiona, not even to Finn and Vivian, despite his comfort speaking to them about almost any other matter, including the ever-widening rift between himself and his wife.

Maximus is now speaking in sentences. He can walk, and he has developed an attachment to a particular stuffed iguana. He favors brightly colored foods over the pallor of potatoes or rice, and he spikes fevers as each of his molars grinds through his gums. The Australian examines through an ever-broadening lens what kind of father, exactly, he'll be. Will he be fun or firm? If a year or two from now he momentarily loses sight of Maximus inside a shop, how in the world will he keep his cool? In the very distant future, if he catches Maximus smoking a cigarette, will his reaction be alienating to Maximus or encouraging of proper health and avoidance of dangerous vices? Will the Australian ever look back upon this particular present moment—say, on the day that Maximus graduates college, or Maximus's wedding day, or the day Maximus himself becomes a father—and mourn his son's receding youth? Or will he celebrate his son's manhood simply and without sentimentality? Will the absence of Lock Jones from the Australian's life handicap him as he undertakes this greatest of all responsibilities, or will his lack of any preconceived notion about fatherhood ultimately prove to be an asset?

It is the answers to these questions that the Australian is seeking as he scrutinizes the photograph, which he does approximately once a week, while Fiona is with the pop star, for example, and Maximus is down for his afternoon nap. Although he tries to restrict himself to a single glance, some days he gets lost deep in his thoughts. His mind wanders and he enters the interior of Lock Jones's consciousness on that long-ago day in the Gibson Desert. He imagines the intensity with which his father must have focused on the task at hand in order to scan the rock face for viable handholds despite the punishing sun, the many spectators, and the physical exhaustion that undoubtedly burned, wretched and caustic, in every fiber of his muscles. There were things Lock must have been accustomed to telling himself when faced with such a challenge—inspirational, steeling—but what where they?

The Australian's mother had related stories of some of Lock's previous *fiascoes*, as she'd called them: skydiving in New Zealand, bungee jumping in Thailand, swimming with great white sharks off the Ivory Coast. The Australian believes that, while Lock was alive, he existed on two separate planes. There was the unavoidable and lusterless realm of the ordinary world, and then there was some dazzling alternate dimension, a vibrant zone where a man like the Australian's father could exist authentically, impugning the limitations of human flesh and bone.

As Maximus's motor skills and teeth and personality emerge, the Australian dwells with increasing frequency upon his father—once estranged, now dead—and is haunted by the same unanswerable questions that once lurked in the dark periphery of his otherwise happy childhood.

That he cannot speak to his wife about his growing fixation on his deceased father the Australian considers par for the course. Thinking of their two lives—Fiona's and his—he recalls a pair of silver-dollar-sized turtles that he has seen for sale on the crowded streets of Chinatown. The turtles, delicate and colorful, reside side by side in their own tiny plastic boxes in twin puddles of green-tinged water. The Australian would like to believe that, despite their squalid living conditions, the turtles find solace and fellowship—even hope—through the algae-streaked walls of their plastic habitats.

Marriage has become lonely and discomfiting, presumably for both parties, but also sustainable. It does not occur to the Australian to stray, nor does he contemplate leaving. His loyalty is not, as Finn and Vivian have implied during more than one conversation, merely a factor of the Australian's love of Maximus or his desire to keep the family intact for the child's sake. In response to his friends' assumptions, the Australian insists that he still loves Fiona, her oddness and quick wit, her sureness and grace as a mother, her quiet yet unwavering self-confidence.

These days he even admires her unremitting patience and loyalty to the pop star, who is now undergoing intensive outpatient treatment for micropsia, which has a drastically distorting effect on visual perception and is also sometimes referred to as Alice in Wonderland Syndrome. Thorough investigation by a team of internationally renowned specialists has traced the affliction's onset to the pop star's recent spirit journey to the Peruvian Amazon, during which, under the guidance of a shaman, she consumed an unknown quantity of a psychedelic root brew called Ayahuasca, or "vine of the souls." Ever since, everything big has, to her, looked tiny. A bus may, for instance, appear to the pop star to be the size of a caterpillar. What initially registers as a mechanical pencil may in fact be a skyscraper. In the face of this distressing and possibly career-ending development, Fiona has been endlessly supportive of her employer and friend. The Australian's distance from his wife gives him an increasingly panoramic perspective, enabling him to value her admirable traits more than ever before. One day, while listening to Fiona describe a tragic game of Pickup Stix she recently played with the pop star, part of the prescribed rehabilitation regimen, the Australian has a bizarre realization: his enlarged perspective on his wife is essentially an inversion of micropsia. He's got selective *macropsia*—Gulliverian vision. But there seems to be no rehabilitation for him, nothing to relieve the stress and anxiety he feels as a result of Fiona's remoteness.

Still, he believes this sad phase of their marriage will soon reach its nadir, at which time he and Fiona will be launched into circumstances vastly superior in every way. An optimist, he believes that if dreams are both possible and desirable, they will become reality. A chance for a new happiness with Fiona is possible. The making of joyous family memories, ones that Maximus will recall with fondness and gratitude for the rest of his long and fabulous life, is possible. Winning Fiona's affection once again, the love that the Australian took for granted and for which he now waits quietly, faithfully, is possible. The universe, the Australian reminds himself each night— while Fiona, in bed beside him, inhabits her own vast and secret umwelt—will ultimately favor happiness.

Both the Australian and Fiona forget their seven-year wedding anniversary until it is almost dinnertime. They have just put Maximus to bed and are sitting in the living room watching TV when Fiona remembers. "How silly is that?" she says. "Seven years. It completely slipped my mind."

"Mine too," says the Australian, speaking in what he hopes is a neutral tone. He is both relieved that she isn't angry and nervous that something might now be expected of him.

"We could try to find a babysitter," says Fiona. "Do something fun. It's been forever since we've done—well, anything, really. We might not be able to find anyone, but it's worth a shot. Right?"

It is a Friday. The Australian does not want to sit in a crammed restaurant or bar, does not feel like moving from the couch upon which he is sitting, does not like the hopefulness that has brightened Fiona's face. Fiona may be trying to reach out to him, to let go of their troubles and reconnect, but he is suddenly, overwhelmingly tired.

"I doubt we can find a sitter this late," he says. He smiles, and with feigned enthusiasm asks, "How about we just order some takeout? Maybe from the good Indian place—the one with that lamb thing you love?"

Fiona looks crestfallen. "Got it," she says, and exits into the bedroom.

"Love you," he thinks he hears her say.

That night the Australian has a dream that will reoccur every few nights for several weeks. In the dream he toils in the ocean for hours, treading water and then freediving into its cold black depths, capturing lobsters with his naked hands. He struggles to complete the task, his fingers torn to shreds. Finally he collects enough lobsters to serve the dozen or so guests he is expecting for a high-pressure, high-stakes social event that he and Fiona will be hosting at their home later that evening.

The Australian decides to keep the lobsters in a large metal basin on the kitchen table filled with saltwater until it is time to boil them. Here the lobsters struggle, frantically attempting to claw their way up the sides of the basin to freedom, but invariably sliding back into the water. Confident that the lobsters' confinement is complete, the Australian leaves the kitchen. He goes about his business, lulled into forgetfulness by a comforting medley of rituals—helping two-and-a-half-year-old Maximus use his training toilet in the corner of the bathroom, reading him to sleep for his nap, doing the lunch dishes, watering the houseplants, paying bills—and he unwittingly abandons the lobsters altogether.

It is only once the sun begins to set, the sky's hues of orange and red reminiscent of the repigmented shell of a cooked lobster, that it suddenly dawns on the Australian that he may have left them in the basin too long, and they might be dead. He rushes to the kitchen to find them no longer thrashing, and the basin water inexplicably steaming hot and churning like a Jacuzzi. The dark green-blue exoskeletons of those ancient crustaceans are bright red, cracked all along the carapace. The hours of cooking alone certainly must have spoiled the meat, but what's worse is that all of the lobsters are now puffing on cigarettes, inhaling deeply and expelling through their blackening gills—dense, reeking billows of tobacco smoke—rendering them totally unpalatable.

Walking toward them, the Australian sees that the expression on all of their pinched, miniscule faces is unmistakably one of thorough and smug satisfaction. As he thinks of the important guests who will soon arrive expecting a feast, the wheels of his mind spin off their axles, the cold stone of terror lodges itself in his diaphragm, and at precisely the moment in which he is sure that the situation could not be worse, he looks toward the doorway of the kitchen and sees Fiona standing there, looking at him with disgust and a smug satisfaction of her own, smiling sourly as though this were precisely the outcome she expected all along.

Over the next few months, the Australian develops a variety of minor physical ailments. Sometimes, as he sits at the dinner table listening to Fiona talk about the distressed pop star with the tenderness that she seems to lavish on everyone except him, the muscles in the back of his neck braid and stiffen. Pain creeps up and over the top of his head, and by bedtime he is wearing an ill-fitting hat made of pain. Sometimes, when he sees Fiona staring bleary-eyed into space and can't help but imagine the particulars and dimensions of the fantasy she may be inhabiting—say, a fantasy in which her husband has more to offer than earnestness and very white teeth—an itchy red rash breaks out inside the crooks of his elbows, behind his knees, and on his neck.

However, the most debilitating of his afflictions is the sickness that has befallen his innards. Three quarters of the time, his colon is so inflamed and rigid that he can easily feel it with his fingers beneath his abdominal muscles if he relaxes them, like a very stale and complicated French pastry. Then, without warning, the spasm suddenly lets up, bringing on a brief period of relief that is quickly eclipsed by a calamitous monsoon of the gut.

"Why don't you see a doctor?" asks Fiona, to which he replies, "Because."

The Australian has a fundamental distrust of the medical profession. He feels both proud and irritated by this attitude—proud because he is taking a stand about something, and irritated because he inherited this particular stance from his mother.

While the Australian was growing up, his mother blamed most of his difficulties, however trivial—from his refusal to memorize his multiplication tables to his strong dislike of coriander—on vaccines, and by association the establishment that administered them. This started when, soon after he began primary school, Margaret joined a knitting circle, the members of which persuaded her that she should have breastfed the Australian at least until kindergarten, and that her premature weaning of him at six months, in combination with the pernicious vaccines, would undoubtedly doom him to eternal sickliness. The only way to avoid such a fate was to aggressively pursue balance and bodily harmony through what they called "pre-healing."

Margaret took to these women and their convictions instantly. She adopted their faith in the Goddess of the Universe, their earthy manner of dress, and their concurrence that she had a rare silver aura, portending an imminent spiritual awakening. She was introduced to healers whose methods were derived from those of the Pygmies and the Native Americans and of course the Aborigines. Simultaneously, she terminated her relationship with Western medicine.

The one time she deemed the Australian in need of a doctor's care was on the afternoon of his only seizure, the result of inhaling the contents of several helium balloons in the aisle of a grocery store. When a store manager called an ambulance, Margaret surrendered to what she would later describe as the fraudulent authority of the medics. The Australian received a single dose of anticonvulsant medication in the emergency room and was released. Otherwise, aside from the annual physical required by the Board of Studies, she only took the Australian to Ayurvedics, homeopaths, psychics, aromatherapists, and iridologists. As an adult, he has never had cause to interact with health professionals of any stripe, although before he met Fiona he slept a few times with a Reiki practitioner—a French Canadian with a Boston Terrier and an underbite, whom he once discovered stealing silverware from his kitchen drawer. All his life the Australian has been exceedingly healthy and thus, when he finally concedes that this digestive malady is not going away on its own and becomes willing to seek professional advice, it will be his first-ever visit to a New York doctor.

The Australian makes an appointment with one Dr. Moskovitz. The doctor comes recommended by Finn, whose mild, adult-onset narcolepsy the doctor successfully treated using a cocktail of weekly B-vitamin injections, daily ice baths, and a rigorous amphetamine regimen. Finn describes Dr. Moskovitz as a "saint" and a "visionary," and although the Australian is skeptical, Finn's praise carries more weight that anyone else's could.

The office is located in the ground floor of a thirty-three-story residential building in Alphabet City on the Lower East Side. The waiting room is all earth tones accented by three large Chinese porcelain vases filled with blooming tiger lilies. Sitting on a wicker loveseat, breathing in the fragrant air, the Australian feels his prejudices beginning to pop one by one like soap bubbles in the air around his head.

After a few minutes' wait, a robust elderly Russian woman leads him into a small examination room. Soon after, Dr. Moskovitz enters, smelling of sweet pipe smoke.

"My mother," he says, smiling sheepishly, gesturing toward the door through which the receptionist has just exited.

He takes the Australian's history, asking not just about his physical health but his life in general, listening—head cocked to the side,

eyes squinting, jotting notes on a yellow legal pad—with what appears to be fascination.

The Australian talks about the holistic treatments, his devotion to
football and cricket growing up, his immigration a decade ago, and
the few minor injuries he sustained as an amateur traceur. He believes
he now understands Finn's fondness for Dr. Moskovitz, who delves
into the Australian's history with tender intrigue, as if gently teasing
apart the delicate chain of a tangled necklace. Before the Australian
knows it he is detailing his reoccurring dream about the lobsters. He
hasn't given it much thought, but suddenly it seems relevant. And
so he is disheartened to notice that, as the minutes tick by, the doctor's attention seems to wane. His posture slackens. His note-taking
diminishes, and then comes to a halt. The Australian is embarrassed
that he ever thought his dream would matter to anyone other than
himself. Nonetheless, he finishes telling it.

"You have quite an imagination," says Dr. Moskovitz, glancing for a third or fourth time at the clock above the examination
table. "Vivid indeed. Well, let me prescribe something for sleep. That
should be of some help to you. As for the digestive troubles, I recommend stress reduction and some kind of relaxation practice. Have
you ever considered meditation?"

The Australian nods.

As the doctor moves briskly and rather roughly through the
physical examination, the Australian wants to ask him how emotions
could have such profound influence over his digestion. Moreover he
wants to know why love hurts so much, what he was really meant
to be in this life, and what or whom the lobsters may represent. He
feels foolish for mistaking this medical man for the kindly healers
of his youth. He worries that his perception of the doctor's initial

fascination may have somehow been an invention of his own mind. He wonders if he could possibly be that desperate, that deluded, that needy and fragile.

Then, in an instant, he feels something new: yearning for his mother. As if the Australian's ribcage is an old guitar upon whose long-neglected strings a sorrowful chord has just been strummed, the hollows of his body now reverberate on the loneliest frequency. A wave of grief overtakes him, and he is only slightly aware of Dr. Moskovitz as he clicks his retractable pen closed, offers the Australian a practiced nod of the head, and darts noiselessly out the door.

The Australian is vaguely pleased that Maximus's third birthday has fallen on a beautiful day, a bright and chilly Friday, the first day that feels like autumn. While Fiona and Maximus are eating breakfast, the Australian excuses himself and writes a long email to his mother. He apologizes for discouraging her attempts to visit and for being uncommunicative. He also recounts the ten and a half years, his time in New York. The Catholic rite of confession has always held great appeal for him, and somehow writing out his own history gives him the feeling he has always imagined the parishioner must enjoy—a solemn unburdening giving way to an exhilarating sensation of cleanliness. But his excitement quickly burns down to its embers, and by the time Maximus's birthday festivities are about to start, the Australian is depleted.

Fiona has organized the party to be attended by six children, featuring Pin the Tail on the Donkey, kids' music on the stereo, red velvet cake, and tea for the parents. When the guests begin to arrive, the Australian struggles to remember which ones he has met before. The parents seem to him like members of some exclusive club that he could never hope to join. So distant does he feel from their world that he cannot tell these slender, wealthy, artistic people from one another. More disconcerting, though, is his struggle—standing numbly beside Fiona, attempting to make small talk with the adults while the children play—to believe that he is actually physically present in his own home. He feels carved from soft stone, something easily and quickly re-contoured by a persistent breeze: alabaster, pumice, chalk.

Over the next few hours, time moves both quickly and slowly at once, in the end leaving the Australian slouched on the couch in a state of cool disassociation. Meanwhile, Fiona seems to be all around him, a gauzy blur as she cleans up from the party.

"I sent my mother an email," says the Australian.

"What's wrong with you?" Fiona asks, gathering plates and napkins from around the living room. The words burst from her, hard staccato.

"It was just this morning. I've invited her here, Fiona. I need her."

Just as it never occurred to him to consult with his wife before extending the invitation, the possibility that she might object to sharing her home with Margaret does not enter his mind now.

"You acted truly bizarre, you know," says Fiona, scrubbing the top of the coffee table with a bright yellow sponge. "You embarrassed me today. You're like a zombie."

The Australian isn't listening. He doesn't know that Fiona is on fire, that the hiss and crackle of those flames are so loud that she can't hear him either. If he is doing something wrong, if he's been doing something wrong for years, he is completely unaware of it. He is curled upon the couch on his side, C-shaped, facing the wall.

"I've got to see my mother," he says. He remembers the omnipresent scent of sandalwood surrounding Margaret, the scent of everything she has recently come to symbolize: safety, history, and wholeness. "She will help me figure things out."

There is a long silence. He turns to look at Fiona, tears in his eyes, but she is no longer in the room.

Two days pass and the Australian has yet to hear back from his mother. He checks his email hourly. Possible scenarios flood his mind, various explanations for her silence, ranging from hurt feelings to natural disasters to computer trouble. Meanwhile Fiona is gliding quickly along some new track. Since Maximus's birthday, she seems to have assumed a posture of surrender vis-à-vis the Australian, as though she's released her grip on everything that was hurting her and now stands watching, blissfully indifferent, as all her troubles float up into the sky. Preoccupied with his mother, the Australian pays little mind to the shift in Fiona's attitude, except to conclude that it is for the best. When after five days of obsessively monitoring his inbox he has yet to receive a reply, he again broaches the topic of Margaret's visit with Fiona. She is dreamily peeling the clear plastic wrapper off some string cheese, and she freezes for a few seconds. As the Australian speaks, she looks at him with a detached kind of pity, as though he were a child on the subway selling broken candy bars out of a shoebox.

"Sounds nice," she says and resumes eating, slowly peeling off one strip of cheese, then another, and placing them neatly upon her tongue.

Another day goes by, and another, and the Australian begins to doubt whether his email even went through. Then, on the kind of windy morning when bits of trash swirl in miniature cyclones along the streets, he logs into his email to find a message from a woman named Deedee, who identifies herself as Margaret's flatmate.

"We have only just read your email," she writes. "Your mother is ill and unable to compose a response. While we hope for a speedy recovery, it will be quite some time before she can travel. She wants to see you desperately. We would love to have you for however long you can manage."

What is wrong with his mother? How serious is her condition? Who is Deedee, and why is she privy to his private correspondence?

What the Australian doesn't wonder is whether or not he will go to Melbourne. Not only will he make the trip, he will leave as soon as possible. Pulled by his rekindled desire for his mother's love, his need to redeem himself in relation to her, and his nostalgia for Australia itself, there is simply no choice to be made.

The Australian responds to Deedee, saying he'll be in Melbourne shortly, but that since he will be joined by his wife and son, he will find his own lodgings. Also, he inquires about the nature of his mother's illness. While he again waits for a response, he buys three plane tickets to Melbourne and secures a sublet through Internet classifieds. This leaves him with four days to convince Fiona to come with him to Melbourne, a task he supposes will be easy. In the face of his mother's unnamed illness and the disturbances in his marriage, a kind of mania has set in. He reasons that this is a family matter. He remembers how, in the days before Maximus was born, he used to regale Fiona with endless stories about his homeland—how the longest fence in the world, the Dingo Fence, runs all the way from Jimbour in Queensland to Great Australian Bight in the south; how he once witnessed his mate lose a third of his surfboard to the jaws of a bull shark in the swells at Bondi Beach; how at age seven he wandered off alone during a trip to the desert with his mother, and how he was saved from being lost forever by the fortuitous appearance of a young

Aboriginal lad named Darel, who guided him, playfully kicking a deflated basketball all the way, through the forty-five-minute trek back to the campsite.

The Australian is encouraged by his memory of Fiona as a free and adventurous spirit. He figures that while he is tending to his mother, Fiona will take Maximus on the tram to the Melbourne Aquarium and the zoo and all the lovely shops, and when Margaret's health has returned, they can all four go on an excursion to the Gondwana Rainforest. They will take an airboat ride along one of the emerald-gray rivers below the rainforest canopy, see crocodiles basking in the sun, colorful birds, neon-green tree snakes, and all the magnificent flowers blooming along the riverbanks and from the vines that climb up the trees toward the invisible sky.

All of this is exactly what the Australian says to Fiona while she is soaking in an oatmeal and lavender oil bath at the end of yet another long day doing therapy exercises with the pop star. As he is speaking, he interprets her silence as approval, her closed eyes as an indication of how deeply she is envisioning their enchanting future.

"It's not forever," he says at the end of his speech, breathless. "A few months—three months, maybe. What do you say?"

Fiona opens her eyes. Something about her gaze unnerves him, and he cannot maintain eye contact. His focus drifts down to her body, submerged in the cloudy water. He notices that she has become thinner, almost too thin, and he wonders when and why this happened.

"I'm sorry about your mother," Fiona says, her voice soft and sad. "I really am. It's terrible that she's ill, and I understand that you need to see her. But, sweetie, you just—you assume so much. You assume I can just leave my life, and that Maximus and I can pick up and travel halfway around the world at a moment's notice. You assume we have enough money to live abroad for months on end. You assume that the people who depend on me here, my friends and my boss, can get along without me."

She gets up out of the bathtub, her face betraying nothing except fatigue, and wraps herself in a white towel. She takes a few steps toward the Australian where he stands leaning against the sink. She is so close he can smell the lavender-scented steam rising off her skin. He wants to touch her, but he is frozen. She leans in, kisses his cheek, pulls him close.

"I'm sorry," she says. "I'm leaving you."

The Australian meets Finn and Vivian for dinner at an Ethiopian restaurant the night before his departure. Finn and Vivian's relationship has been stable for months now, ever since Finn consigned himself to what he and Vivian call the "French agreement," an arrangement in which both parties of a relationship may discreetly have sex with whomever they fancy. Of course this was all Vivian's idea. While Finn initially found the concept quite upsetting, not hearing about her affairs and also the possibility—as yet unconsummated—that he might have affairs of his own has helped him relax. They both seem to have acclimated nicely.

Before leaving the apartment, the Australian lingered, sobs caught in his throat, in Maximus's bedroom, watching his sleeping son illuminated by a dragonfly nightlight. The reality that the Australian will be spending far less time with his bright-eyed child even once he returns to New York has been slowly sinking in. The pain of this has been consuming him all day, so that he hasn't yet begun to grapple with the other reality—that of his imminent separation from his wife. Fiona has been sleeping on the living room couch. She says she might move into the pop star's brownstone, where she could be most useful to her—helping with all the daily tasks made so difficult by the micropsia. She plans to bring Maximus, too. She has been talking about things like shared custody, selling the apartment, division of furniture.

It is only when the Australian arrives at the overheated restaurant, puffy-eyed and fifteen minutes late, and sees Finn and Vivian gazing lovingly at each other across the table that he is hit by the totality of his loss. He is sickened by his friends' mutual contentment. He allows them to carry the conversation, occasionally nodding, uttering one or two syllables whenever it seems absolutely necessary. After food has been ordered, Vivian begins talking excitedly about a grant she has just received, which will enable her to make her next short film. Entitled *Visions of You*, it will be a fictional series of vignettes in which, through a new kind of national lottery, ordinary people win five-minute conversations with their idols—actors, musicians, athletes, authors, and so forth. She wants to expose both the heartbreak and humor of the moment in which celebrity is replaced by a complex reality. "It's about, you know, the problem—the paradox—of our need for an authentic connection to a fantasy," she says.

The Australian offers his congratulations and manages to feign mild interest, but none of it means anything to him. While he has told his friends about his mother's illness, the specifics of which are still unknown to him, he has said nothing of Fiona's decision. It had been his intention to do so now, but as he struggles to eat his food, washing down each tiny bite with several gulps of water, it is just too much.

"Do you not like the *kitfo*?" says Vivian, sweetly. He knows that she and Finn are probably attributing his distress solely to his mother's sickness. "How about some more *injera*?"

The Australian shakes his head. He wants to jump ship, escape the stuffy restaurant, the food, and most of all his friends. The idea comes to him that he is losing everything and that once he has nothing further loss will be impossible. In that moment, it is all he can manage to hope for. He imagines his life as a blank movie screen across which words flash in big black letters: FUN, PAIN, LOVE, BROKEN, FLYING. The waiter begins to clear away the plates. Without waiting for the check to arrive, the Australian drops a twenty-dollar bill on the table, pecks his two friends on their cheeks, winds through the restaurant, and steps out into the night.

PART THREE

THE AUSTRALIAN WALKS ALONG the streets of Fitzroy, an upscale bohemian neighborhood on Melbourne's Northside.
From airplane to Skybus, and from Skybus to tram, he has
been hauling a heavy duffel bag and a bloated knapsack in which
the photograph of Lock Jones is stowed. He had always hoped his
eventual return to Melbourne would be triumphant. Although the
circumstances of his homecoming are hardly victorious, he is too
fatigued from his journey to flagellate himself as he now reckons he
deserves. Melbourne's Northside was never his home anyway, not
like the Southside—with its bars and discos, mirrored office buildings, and brilliant, glitter-glass sidewalks—where admission to life's
celebration is granted by a smile, a healthy tan, and readiness for action. Surely it would be more painful over there, along the far shore
of the Yarra River—in the shade beneath the arched tree boughs
on the campus of the Australian's alma mater or at some other site
central to his past. Perhaps he ought to go immediately to one of
those places in order to fully experience his own fall from grace. But
these thoughts are quickly replaced by a resurgence of the pressing
need to see his mother, whom he will see to health, and who will
help him retrieve his life.

According to Deedee's first email, she and Margaret share a flat off bustling Gertrude Street. Men ride bicycles in skin-tight jeans and an elderly Bengali man in seersucker shorts chews on the stub of a cigarillo, standing before a card table fanned with classic New Wave LPs. There is a tidy row of cafés with pretty outdoor seating and a vintage clothing consignment shop whose exterior is painted the same happy yellow as the golden wattle, Australia's national flower. Despite the gentrification of Fitzroy over the last few decades, the original Victorian architecture remains, majestic and whimsical, rising up above the storefronts' modern façades. Turning onto a narrow side street, the Australian finds himself standing in front of the old green house where his mother now lives. He pushes the buzzer for flat 1B and prepares to encounter Margaret for the first time in over a decade.

The front door swings open, revealing a short woman. Colorful tattoos span shoulder to wrist, animated by her lean and angular musculature. In an instant, her arms are hugging his waist.

"We are so relieved you've come," she says, her words exhaled against his chest. "I'm Deedee, of course. Let's have a look at you."

One of her pale blue eyes is a glass prosthetic, and she moves with the brittle grace of a retired ballerina. She is wearing a black tank top and a long, flowing white skirt with dime-sized mirrors sewn onto the fabric. All of the tattoos covering her arms depict beautiful women overlapping and intertwined with other beautiful women. Deedee is somewhere around the Australian's own age, maybe a bit younger, her fair skin completely unlined and her bleach blond hair in a disheveled topknot.

The house is divided into separate flats. Deedee leads the Australian along a narrow hallway, stopping in front of the first of three small doors. She looks up into his face.

"Your mother suffers from the butterfly disease," she says, her tone matter of fact.

"The butterfly disease?"

"She is within the cocoon of her spiritual bondage," she says. "But we are working hard every day to break her free."

"But what does that mean? What is her diagnosis?" He looks sharply into her good eye.

"As you know, Margaret's life hasn't always been easy. She's carried burdens from other lifetimes, and they've finally caught up with her. The butterfly disease is her body's manifestation of her relationship to the past—her conflicting wish to escape undesirable situations, and also to keep things as they are."

"I don't understand." The Australian is nearing the point of anger.

Deedee looks upward, as if searching for the right words. Her gaze returns to him.

"Right now, Margaret is weakened by disharmonious energy," she says. "Your mother has a condition of the blood—a natural response, really, to the ancestral sorrows that flow through her veins. I know it's a lot to wrap your head around. It's different for me, I suppose. I'm an Intuitive."

"Has she been to see a doctor?"

"Yes, of course," she says, with a whiff of defensiveness. "We visited two top physicians at the university hospital, and both of them agreed—it is a spiritual matter best dealt with at home."

The Australian cannot fathom any context in which a medical doctor would render such a prognosis. He demands to see his mother immediately, to assess her well-being himself.

Inside the apartment, Deedee leads the Australian through a small living room, over a worn oriental carpet, past three blossoming hibiscus plants, an antique metal birdcage housing an African grey parrot, several bookshelves, and a miniature electronic organ called The Entertainer II, which he recognizes as a relic from Margaret's rendezvous with evangelical Christianity back when he was a teenager. The organ is covered with white candles, lit and at varying stages of melting, their wax flowing like cream over the keyboard and multicolored sound-effect buttons. The rich amber sunrays of early dusk stretch in through a large picture window and shine across the room, and within the columns of light float tiny white clouds of fluff. "Aphrodite is molting," says Deedee.

At the far end of the living room, a narrow corridor leads to a kitchen whose surfaces have been rendered invisible by dozens of canisters, plastic tubs, glass droppers, vials, and tins. Before the kitchen, against the wall of the corridor, is a closed door.

"Your mother is in there." Deedee gestures at the door. "It's our room, but she has it to herself until she gets well. These days I sleep in the spare room, so I'm afraid that means you'll have to sleep on the couch."

"No worries," says the Australian, feeling as though he ought to say something else but unsure of what that might be.

"Well, go on in." She pats his back and returns to the living room.

The Australian grips the crystal knob and opens the door a crack. He is hit by the unmistakable odor of sickness, like dry earth and spoiled milk. His pressing need to be near his mother is replaced by a desire, just as pressing, to flee. Instead, he opens the door all the way. Margaret lies sleeping in a bed in the center of the large room, lit by thin ribbons of golden light penetrating the spaces between the slats of Venetian blinds. The bed is surrounded by houseplants and a humidifier gurgles in the corner. Atop a bedside table, the amethyst interior of a halved geode sparkles.

"Mum," says the Australian. Quietly, slowly, he approaches her.

"You came," she says, smiling dreamily, eyes still shut.

Standing next to her pillow, he detects the bracing scent of sandalwood. Margaret's hair tumbles, mostly silver now but still lustrous, over the white pillowcase. Her face is relaxed and puffy with sleep, so smooth as to be masklike. He takes her hand and her eyes flutter open.

"I've missed you," he says, in a whisper.

"My little lamb."

"I call my son that. I call Maximus little lamb, all the time." Tears fill the Australian's eyes, but he is unsure for whom. "Are you in pain?"

"No, not anymore." She kisses his hand and presses it against the soft warmth of her cheek. "Not now that you're home."

She lets out a sigh, closes her eyes, and is immediately, soundly asleep. The Australian remains kneeling beside her. As night falls, he listens to her inhale and exhale, her breaths deep and slow. He watches her chest rise and fall, fearing that at any moment the movement will stop.

Later that night, over ginger root tea, the Australian sits shaking his leg underneath the kitchen table while Deedee attempts to assuage his fears.

"I understand that it must be frightening to see your mum like this," she says. "You've got to understand that she is in her cocoon stage. She will emerge, and it will happen soon. Even as we sit here, I can sense a new life stirring inside her. She will blossom, dear, and when she does, we will stand in awe of the cosmic power that is your mother."

Much as the Australian wants to be a source of positivity and support, and, more than anything, believe that his mother will recover, he cannot accept Deedee's conception of the illness. He cannot accept that the herbs and powders in the kitchen will cure her. Utterly depleted from his journey and the emotional strain of the evening, he decides that, while Deedee might be insane, the least he can do—for his mother and for the woman with whom, he suspects, she is in love—is to pretend to have faith.

"I'll be here," he says. "I will be here when she gets well."

On a winter evening when the Australian was twelve, his mother helped him complete some homework—not for school, but for a children's creative exploration workshop taught by the poetess wife of her guru at the time. He had been instructed to write about what the word *duende* meant to him.

"Well, what is *duende*?" Margaret asked, sitting on the edge of the Australian's unmade bed.

"Football," he said, arms crossed against his chest.

"Very funny, mister. What does it say on that sheet of paper?"

Occasionally the young Australian found himself moved by his mother's patience and this was one of those times. Yet, as a boy on the brink of his teenage years, he felt compelled to maintain his aloofness.

Slouched at his desk, he read flatly from the Xeroxed sheet of paper provided by the teacher: "*Duende* is the spirit of evocation, soul, and creative expression of which the core elements are irrationality, earthiness, and heightened awareness of death."

"All right," said Margaret. "Read it once more, less like a robot this time."

The Australian complied, enunciating each word to a ridiculous extreme, adding extra syllables and strange inflections.

"Now, close your eyes," said Margaret. "Sit with your *duende*. Feel it rise from the soles of your feet all the way up to the top of your head."

As the Australian pretended to meditate on his own mysterious life force, he could hear his mother breathing deeply, in her nose and out her mouth, and he knew that she was doing it with him. He felt sorry for lacking whatever it was she had.

"I feel it, Mum," he said.

"Yes, darling," Margaret replied, her voice wavering with intensity. "I feel it too."

Sipping his tea, listening to Deedee go on about his mother's imminent emergence, the Australian once again experiences himself as lacking some fundamental quality or capacity, the key to what his mother needs him to be. More than ever, he needs his mother's optimism. Even if he can't share it, he needs her belief in his spirit's irrevocable worth. He decides that, given the chance, he will spend whatever time he has with Margaret on her terms.

"I'm not going anywhere until she gets better," says the Australian.

"I knew you'd be here," says Deedee, nodding as if to music, a song she's heard a thousand times. "You're in the right place."

The Australian lets his eyes defocus and returns to the memory, but he can't recall how that exchange with Margaret concluded. What he does remember is that it was one of the most perfect moments they ever shared—not because he ultimately attained any real understanding of his spiritual self, but because, eyes closed and breathing in unison, they'd both pretended he could.

Once the conversation about Margaret's affliction has ended, the Australian asks Deedee many questions. Sitting across the kitchen table, her slight frame wrapped in a magnolia-print silk kimono, she delivers a frank synopsis of what she calls her "odyssey." In her youth, she was a contortionist, but a mediocre one, and lost her job with a second-rate circus after dislocating a hip during her act. Afterward, having become addicted to painkillers, she moved to the outskirts of Perth, where she made a living selling black-market chemical hand-warming packets, cigarettes, and miniature bottles of Czech vodka to the men servicing trains at the Kewdale Freight Terminal. It was in that industrial wasteland that she got hooked on heroin and, in a desperate moment, after the boarding house where she had been living for two miserable years was condemned, agreed to be taken in by Kewdale's roundhouse foreman, a burly Taurus named Stephan—a recovering alcoholic who wrote down twenty things he was grateful for every day. Stephan helped her kick heroin, introduced her to a variety of meditation practices, and assisted her in securing a legitimate job as the rail station janitor.

The ease with which Deedee talks about her past impresses the Australian more than the stories themselves, and he finds himself revising his initial conception of her. In order to have survived, she must be resilient and thick-skinned, which is more than the Australian can say for himself. She is like the girls who used to surf, despite the dangerous riptides, at Gunnamatta beach—girls who seemed to have seen and experienced everything, girls who roved in all-girl packs, girls who wouldn't give him or his mates the time of day—and he wants her to like him.

"How did you meet my mother?" he asks, embarrassed that he hadn't already posed the obligatory question.

Deedee smiles, a bright glint coming into her good eye, and clasps her hands upon the tabletop. "Once I'd been clean for a year, my parents invited me up to Melbourne for Easter. While I was in town, I visited a meditation group and it was there that I met Margaret."

"Makes sense," he says. "That's nice."

The Australian knows he really ought to be more interested in his mother's romance, but he keeps thinking back to Deedee's account of her life as a drug addict. The tale seemed to energize her, as though it were not her own life she had been recounting but the plot of a favorite movie or novel. Perhaps such exquisite detachment from painful memories might one day be possible for him. He takes a silent inventory of the sources of his pain. He imagines laying a bouquet of flowers atop his father's gravestone. Even if he knew where his father was buried, the act would be insufficient. The Australian's ever-deepening wound would not be filled or closed that easily.

He interrupts Deedee while she is explaining the fundamentals of the tantra—how one might tap into *prāna*, the energy that flows through the universe, and use it to fulfill his or her every desire—and asks her how she was able to cast away the burdens of the life she had led in Perth. She considers him, perhaps contemplating his motive for asking the question, and ultimately she seems satisfied by her appraisal.

"Today is all we've got," she says. "The past belongs to someone else, someone who is no longer me."

The Australian feels that they are speaking two different languages. Her language is familiar by way of his mother, and yet, as always, it remains beyond his translational capacities. His exasperation with her resurges.

"If all we have is today, what are we supposed to do with it?" asks the Australian.

"We've just got to keep moving," Deedee replies. "Trudging along the road to joyous destiny."

The Australian wakes early the next morning, achy from sleeping on the sagging living room couch, roused by the parrot who is shouting from across the room. "Love ya!" says Aphrodite, her voice forceful yet muted, like a yell trapped in a soup can. "Hello! Love ya!" The Australian's chest tightens with the thought of Maximus, who would no doubt be fascinated by the bird, and who by now must be reeling from the shockwaves of his father's departure, those first pangs of hurt amplified by his inability to comprehend their source. He wonders how his absence has affected Fiona, whether she thinks of him constantly or has banished him from her thoughts. Has a dense mass of grief lodged just above her navel? It may be wrong to wish suffering upon her, but if his absence doesn't pain her, why would she ever take him back?

The bedroom doors are shut. Lemony morning light fills the living room. As if she has decided that, having properly disturbed the Australian, her work is done, Aphrodite quiets, and the apartment is silent. The Australian's knapsack rests on the floor beside the couch. From within one of its front pockets he removes his watch. It reads 6:08, and it takes him a long moment to realize that the time on the digital display is p.m., not a.m., because he didn't reset it upon his arrival.

Using a calling card purchased at the airport, he dials his New York apartment. The phone rings four times, and then the answering machine clicks on. He anticipates the queer experience of listening to his own voice from halfway around the world. Instead, it is Fiona's voice he hears. Her tone is chipper, every syllable a projectile. "Please leave your name and number," she says, "and I'll return your call."

The Australian leaves a short message, addressing only his son. "Thinking of you every moment, sending love," he says. "Be good to your mum. See you soon, kiddo."

Replacing the phone in its cradle, he becomes aware of Deedee, who has walked across the apartment and entered the living room. He opens his mouth to apologize for waking her, but she speaks first.

"There is something you've got to see," she says. "Come quickly. It's all happening much sooner than I expected."

The Australian follows her to his mother's room. Margaret is standing facing the window, looking out through the incandescent morning light onto the street below. The old proverb returns: "Keep your eyes on the sun, and you cannot see the shadows." Margaret looks over her shoulder at him, smiling serenely.

"What a brilliant morning," she says, her voice pure and resonant, like a cello confidently bowed. "Shall we get out and soak in this glorious sunlight?"

All day, the Australian follows his mother through the streets of Fitzroy and beyond, trying not to worry about her health, trying to dismiss the ominous haze he perceives casting a dark veil over her sudden vitality. Deedee is with them, marveling at Margaret's spectacular and instantaneous resurrection. She flits in and out of bookshops, bakeries, and parks and calls briefly at the homes of several astonished friends, gliding through the city, halting without warning to take note of seemingly unremarkable details—a dusty sparrow pecking at some crumbs, a candy bar wrapper dragged across the street by a breeze, a teenage girl unlocking her bicycle from a tree.

The Australian recalls Vivian's descriptions of the Annual Starship Symposium. Having so recently been touched by death's cool hand, Margaret appears to have acquired a unique expertise about the world, a special kind of perception similar to that of the conference-goers. Like the precisely honed madness of those scientists gazing upward, perceiving what lies beyond the borders of the known universe, at every turn Margaret displays an ability to decode the world's mundanities, to mentally polish every stranger's dull face, every dog halfheartedly straining against its leash, every ordinary chemist shop's window display, and every tawny tuft of grass growing up through a crack in the sidewalk into resplendence.

Her ambition is undefined, the forces propelling her unknowable yet nonetheless contagious. As the hours pass, the ominous haze surrounding her is relinquished to the future, of which the Australian, in the midst of his mother's flourishing, can no longer conceive. Just as he does with Maximus, he finds himself seeking out beauty along with his mother, trying to see the world through her eyes. Yet, although he sets his sharpest gaze upon the urban landscape, the form and motion of Margaret manifest beauty most.

In a secondhand bookstore, she pores over cookbooks, her back pressed against the bookcases. "These scones," she says. "Orange zest, lemon zest, cardamom. I've got to try this recipe." On the street, she laughs like a schoolgirl at the sight of a blue balloon soaring overhead. She looks up to watch the balloon pass by, and for a moment it appears as though light is emanating from her face, a preternatural attempt to meet the sun halfway.

Next, the Australian and Deedee follow her down a winding residential street, finally arriving at a small brown house. Margaret rings the doorbell, and when her friend Andrew—a middle-aged house painter from her drum circle—answers, the two collapse into an embrace.

"I can't believe it's you," he says. "But it really is. Are you sure you're well enough to be out?"

"I feel just divine," says Margaret, cradling her friend's face in her palms.

"I have no words," says Andrew. "I'm speechless."

In a nearby park, the face of a teenage runaway named Vickie brightens with recognition as Margaret hands her a white paper bag containing two freshly baked brioches. At the florist's, their last stop, Margaret emerges from behind shelves of blooming flowers with a new plant for the apartment, a voluptuous potted *Hippeastrum*. On the way home, Margaret grabs hold of Deedee's and the Australian's hands. She studies their faces, one and then the other, with the shine of love in her eyes, and the Australian thinks, *She is beautiful, she is my mother, and she is alive.*

Early in the evening, the Australian helps Margaret into bed. Her exhaustion came on the instant they returned to the flat.

"She is fading now," says Deedee, when the Australian leaves his mother's bedside, briefly, to pour them each a cool glass of pomegranate juice. "I can feel it, darling. Here," she says, jabbing her own sternum with her thumb.

The Australian tells himself that Deedee is crazy, that she knows nothing. Something infantile surges up, a pure need and panic that only nearness to his mother can soothe. He wants Deedee to leave him and Margaret alone, which he hopes she will intuit as she seems to everything else. And she does. After he returns to the bedroom, he doesn't set eyes on Deedee until morning.

The conversation between the Australian and his mother spans the many years of their separation. They talk about America—New York, California, Arizona—places she has never been. They talk about her affection for Deedee, which deepened profoundly when, soon after moving in with Margaret, Deedee donated her left eyeball to her younger brother, who suffered from inoperable bilateral cataracts. They discuss Maximus—his budding musical talent, which became apparent after Fiona brought home a ukulele, his unfailing kindness to other children at the park, and his adventurous palate, a trait Margaret says he inherited from his father. Margaret swoons over a laminated picture of Maximus from the Australian's wallet.

The briskness and buoyancy of their chatter evokes in the Australian a feeling that might actually be faith. Not only is everything *going* to be OK, but perhaps it always has been. Maybe, now that the house of his heart has been stripped down to the drywall and he has returned to the place of his beginnings, he is developing a burgeoning belief in something greater, the capacity for spiritual insight his mother always wished for him. But when Margaret finally asks about Fiona and he starts to describe the fulfilling and peaceful life waiting for him back in New York, the Australian knows his hopes for himself are unfounded. How idiotic to think it would be so easy, so simple to become a better person just because he needs to.

"Fiona is wonderful," he says. "She makes me feel like the luckiest man in the world, every day. I can't imagine where I'd be without her, and Maximus too."

"Your happiness brings me such joy." Margaret's eyes gleam.

"Thank you, Mum."

Her expression is one of absolute openness, which used to infuriate the Australian. That nakedness always struck him as manipulative, inciting an unfair sense of responsibility in him even as a child. With her expressions and her posture, even the way she fiddled with the fringe of hair at the end of her braid, she gave him the knowledge that her serenity derived from his actions, and that therefore—without ever agreeing to it—he had been given the charge of keeping her whole. Even now, as she gazes adoringly at him from her sickbed, he feels an unsettling tinge of aggression. How easy it would be to ruin this moment with a few honest words.

The Australian runs his fingers through his hair, steadies his breath, lets it go. "It looks like there's a job at an excellent nonprofit waiting for me, whenever I decide to return," he says. "It's a solid organization. Good people, socially conscious. I couldn't be any happier."

His lies are bold and come to him without effort or even the slightest anxiety. Is this what lying was like for Fiona? No. Fiona's lies were ornaments—pretty fandangle.

After Margaret falls asleep, dreams roll across her face. The Australian hopes she is pushing Maximus on a swing, drinking a flat white with Fiona, taking in the downtown skyline from the southward-facing window of the New York apartment. He doesn't worry that he will be found out, that time will reveal him as a fraud. Pondering his lack of anxiety at the possibility that one day his real life will be exposed— loveless, estranged, and impoverished—he becomes conscious of what he knows to be true: his mother will never see any of it.

The next morning, the Australian is woken by frightening vocalizations issuing from his mother's bedroom—animal sounds, like the mewing of a feral cat injured or in heat. Without daring to open his mother's bedroom door, he wakes Deedee, who rushes to Margaret's bedside with a basin of warm water and washcloth. After a few minutes, the Australian walks down the corridor and looks into the bedroom. He stands in the doorway silently as Deedee nurses his mother, who is soothed by the presence of her lover. It finally occurs to him what Deedee must have meant when she told him that the doctors had deemed Margaret's condition a spiritual matter, best dealt with on her own terms. "There's nothing we can do for her beyond palliative care," they must have said. "Perhaps she will be more comfortable at home."

At seventeen, the Australian was pummeled off his surfboard by a rogue wave. Like a pinwheel, he spun and tumbled underwater, deeper and deeper, dragged by the claws of the undercurrent until he no longer knew which way was up. As Margaret mutters her dreams, perspiring and restless with fever, the same terror at his mortality returns. He is only abstractly aware of fear for his mother and gratitude for Deedee's competence. The scene playing out in the bedroom takes on an alien quality, the two women like words repeated into strangeness. Suffocation is rapidly taking hold of him. The butter-colored walls of the flat seem to be sucking in, compressing the air into some denser and more oppressive gas, exerting pressure on every inch of his body.

"I need a coffee," he says.

From her chair at Margaret's bedside, Deedee nods without meeting his gaze.

"Back in a flash."

The Australian intends to get some fresh air and promptly return, but once he reaches the corner coffee shop he is propelled onward. The warm breeze is a drug of mercy. The farther he gets from his mother and Deedee and the dark forces bearing down on them, the higher he feels and the faster he walks. With each long stride, he becomes more immersed in a series of preposterous visions.

There he is, trekking alone into the virtually unpopulated central region of the Outback, a place they call the Never Never, where no one will ever find him. There he is, freediving, BASE jumping, spearfishing, skydiving, whitewater kayaking, parachuting, skateboarding, crocodile wrestling, bullfighting, drag racing, hang gliding over the mouth of an active volcano.

There he is answering a call on his cell phone from an unknown number, learning that Lock Jones is still alive and right there on the other end of the line, that he faked his own death to avoid prosecution for some tax-related crime and has been tirelessly searching for the Australian.

There he is, spotting Finn, who has flown to Melbourne to surprise him, walking toward him just half a block ahead.

There he is, fucking a series of historically unfuckable people: his secondary school girlfriend, who has existed in his mind as willfully and eternally virginal; Elijah the coke dealer, about whom the Australian rarely thinks, but whose refusal to agree to the Australian's propositions had, time and again, sent him into the pits of shame; and a certain redheaded lifeguard whose slate-gray eyes, despite the Australian's attempts in late adolescence to simply have a conversation with her, had remained focused on the sea so immovably that he wondered more than once whether the grayness of those eyes might owe to their constant communion with waves and fog.

There he is, seated at the judges' table of a parkour tournament in which Luc Chevalier is a competitor, and after observing a slight flaw in Luc's technique, the Australian is forced to award the gold medal to Luc's archrival.

There he is, completing the Sunday crossword, square after square, without the slightest hesitation.

Having walked for several hours in a series of aimless loops, he has traversed the city and is now in St. Kilda—Southside. He passes by a Catholic church, and then comes his imagined seduction of a sweet young nun—not one whose disadvantaged circumstances have driven her to profess a religious calling for the sake of survival, but one who has made an honest choice, who truly feels that she has, through her sacred vows, achieved absolute intimacy with Jesus Christ Himself, and who has therefore made heartfelt and willing promises of chastity—and yet who is, despite the threat of eternal hellfire, unable to resist the Australian.

Then, walking in the direction of the harbor, he passes a bank—and there he is, making just the right investment at exactly the right time, becoming a man who no longer has to depend on his wife financially, who need no longer worry about his son's looming education at a private school, who does not refer to a particular credit card as "the good card," and who can visit the dentist on a whim. And better yet, a person who travels by private jet, whose mind is imprinted with Technicolor impressions of Canary Island fireflies and the iridescent jellyfish of the Caspian Sea, who is compassionate yet unyielding when it comes to the demands he makes on domestic help, and whose every eccentricity is viewed as a lark, a hoot, a distinction worthy of celebration.

Now he is winning at hand-to-hand combat against three of the pop star's most muscular backup dancers while Fiona cheers him on. Now he is standing at water's edge watching penguins pull themselves from the waves and waddle to their nests among the rocks of the breakwater. He is glowing and golden, pure and unending luminosity, a permanent fixture in an otherwise dimming universe, steadfast amidst the transience of stars, which eventually burn out, and planets, which eventually crash into stars—an infinite spectacle of light and glory.

At the harbor of St. Kilda, the Australian sits on a bench facing the sea, watching people stream up and down the boardwalk, his own imaginings of their lives radiating from their bodies. Many of them are Western tourists, energized by the novelty of summer weather in December. They have children, or they are on their honeymoons, or they are eighteen and in the middle of their gap years—dingy under the eyes from too much partying and sleeping in crowded youth hostels, intent on packing in maximum adventure before the start of university in six months' time. All of them are on the outer rim of their experience, snapping pictures with cameras and cell phones of the penguins, the cafés, the juggler, the landscape watercolorist, the swooping gulls. In days or hours, they will exchange their currency, present their passports, and lose these moments to the various irritations of traveling long distances by plane. Back in their homes, they will consider themselves richer for their travels, broadened and smoothed by their exposure to foreignness, but their memories of those strange moments in Australia, the ones that made them feel so alive, will dry out, flake off, and fall away.

A woman approaches, trailed by her husband, who pushes their identical twin daughters, close in age to Maximus, in a double stroller.

"Excuse me," she says, her accent from New Zealand. "We're trying to find Luna Park. Are we nearby?"

The Australian frequented Luna Park as a teenager. It all comes back: the fried-food smells, the ornate carnival decorations, people screaming on the amusement park rides, the singe of fresh paint in his nostrils on a day when groundskeepers were touching up the park's entrance, an arch formed by the open mouth of some nameless sun god with silver-gold rays spiking like a crown from its brow. He still knows exactly how to get to Luna Park.

That he has remained recognizably Australian after all this time, despite everything that has happened in the many years since he left home—that the couple has deduced as much, that nothing in his appearance or demeanor makes them question it—ignites in him a deep anger.

"Sorry," he says, faking an American accent. "I don't know where that is." Fiona has many times laughed at his American accent, which he only ever attempted jokingly, but now he is trying his very best. "You should ask someone else. I'm just a tourist."

The woman smiles at what she believes to be her mistake, and the family strolls out toward the center of the boardwalk. Over the next few minutes, they approach several more people and ask for directions, until they receive a satisfactory answer. The wife and the husband and the stroller carrying their little girls get smaller and smaller, the white sun shining on their backs.

The Australian returns to Deedee and Margaret's flat at dusk. He doesn't have a key. Before ringing the buzzer, he hesitates on the steps at the front door. His mind churns out excuses that he might offer for his prolonged absence—getting terribly lost, running into an old friend, sudden illness or injury, falling victim to a mugger—but there is no event he can conjure that would justify an all-day disappearance. The circumstances could only be made worse by a flimsy and transparent untruth. He wipes sweat from his upper lip and presses the buzzer. Several minutes pass.

There are only two reasons Deedee might not be home. The first is that Margaret reached such a level of agony that Deedee could no longer manage, despite her claims regarding natural salves and potions, and took Margaret to a hospital. The second is that the Australian's mother is dead.

As he pivots away from the door, prepared to rush to a nearby emergency room, it swings open. He turns to face Deedee, expecting her to lash out at him in anger for staying out all day. Instead, she looks upon him with pity.

"How is she?" he asks.

"She's resting," says Deedee. "She is between worlds—this one and the next."

The Australian stares down at the patch of cement between his feet and hers, willing it to crack, to split open and swallow him.

"Come here, love," says Deedee, curling one arm around his waist.

She raises her free hand up to his head and begins to smooth his hair, tousled and gritty from the ocean's salty breeze. Never has the Australian felt more pathetic than he does now, in the face of Deedee's generosity and compassion. Her kindness is infinitely worse than any scorn or judgment. He feels himself plummeting.

"My wife left me," he says. "I miss her. And my son, Maximus."

He smashes into the cold and unforgiving floor of a deep, black pit.

"I don't know how long your mother will be with us," says Deedee. She releases him from the embrace and squeezes his shoulder. "She still has her lucid moments. You'll want this time with her, to make your peace."

Upon entering the flat, the Australian walks straight to the loo. He washes his hands and examines his face in the mirror. Sunburn is blooming across his nose and cheeks, wrinkles reaching out from the creases of his eyelids and etched across his forehead. They seem to be deepening, sinking into themselves like drought-season riverbeds. A morbid transformation seems to be taking place before his very eyes. In just a few days, he will turn thirty-four. He shuts off the light and exits the bathroom. The exertion required to move down the corridor to his mother's room is a ruthless act of will. Making his way toward her, he envisions slow-motion footage of a stone pitched through a window.

At the doorway of Margaret's bedroom, everything speeds up. The Australian is standing at his mother's bedside, next to Deedee who sits in a chair, which in the very next moment is empty. The Australian sits in the chair. Margaret is awake, her eyes sparkling blue, her face disfigured by swelling. It is the chill of her skin that makes him aware he is holding her hand.

"I should have been here today," he says. He wishes time could be slowed, that it didn't have to be this way. "I wanted to be with you, Mum."

She brings his hand to her cheek, just as she did on the night of his arrival, now clammy and thick with fluid. "You are here, darling," she says. "I can see you."

"You forgive me too much," says the Australian.

Margaret blinks so slowly that he worries she is falling asleep.

"I remember how scared I was when you were born," she says. "I was terrified of raising a boy. Everything I ever did right as a mother came from the courage you gave me." She cringes. Then she relaxes, exhaling slowly. "You have a glow. A special energy."

"I wish that were true," says the Australian.

"Oh, it's true. When you were six years old, just starting primary school, one of your teachers said to me, 'Your little lad has charisma.' It's a funny thing to say about a small child, but I understood completely. She was talking about the spirit of discovery that lives in you. It takes bravery to shine in that way."

"I wish I were brave, Mum," he says.

"Of course you're brave. Just like your father."

Margaret's breath gets snagged on something. As she is seized by a fit of coughing, the Australian tries not to grimace at the sound, her struggle against a surge of bronchial excretions.

When she has settled, he gets out of the chair and kneels on the floor by her bed. Through the quilt that covers her, he presses his face into her shoulder.

"You used to tell me those Aboriginal proverbs," he says, close enough to her ear that he must whisper.

"Do you remember any?" asks Margaret.

"Of course," he says. "Stare into the sun, and you will not see the shadows."

"I'd forgotten that one. I haven't thought about it in years. Do you remember the one I used to say to you before bed?"

The Australian closes his eyes. An image rises to the surface: his mother seated on the edge of his bed, her long braid draped over one shoulder, smiling down at him. He remembers the smell of the sandalwood oil that rose up off her skin, the same scent that he smells now.

"I can't remember," he says.

Margaret's breathing slows and deepens, as though she is balanced on the edge of sleep. In a whisper, she recites the proverb, the last coherent words she speaks to the Australian: "Those who lose dreaming are lost."

At fourteen the Australian found a handwritten letter from Margaret to Lock Jones, still attached to a pad of paper on the kitchen table. In the letter, she expressed to Lock that her financial circumstances were precarious and asked him to send money. In that moment, the Australian had decided to believe the letter was nothing more than an exercise for his mother, a private gesture. For as long as he could remember, his mother had prayed to countless gods. Might not the letter, scrawled in obvious haste, be a similar sort of outcry? Lock Jones was himself a mythical figure, an idol whose likeness the Australian worshipped in the form of the single photograph. Perhaps Margaret felt similarly. Might not she view him as a building block so essential to her universe that she might reach out to him through the ether—by writing the letter, and then perhaps burning it ceremoniously?

Long ago, the Australian committed to the belief that Lock Jones never received any correspondence from Margaret and therefore was not aware of his son's existence. To allow for the possibility that his mother had contact with Lock would have been too much to bear. The question was settled until approximately one week after Lock Jones's death, when the Australian received a phone call from a lawyer, a lady with a nasal voice and a bushie accent, who explained she was reaching out on behalf of his deceased father in order to bestow his inheritance. She refused to explain how she had located him.

At that time, the Australian constructed a scenario in which Lock had some record of his affair with Margaret—a diary entry, perhaps, or a story told to a friend—which ultimately made the Australian findable by association. Twenty-three and alone in New York, the Australian never broached the topic with his mother. However, beneath his manufactured certainty simmered great resentment against her for the possibility that she had indeed sent the letter, that it was one of several, or even many. His unwillingness to accept this possibility added to his reasons for distancing himself from her. He let the rift expand until it was too much to take.

Now, at Margaret's bedside, the events leading up to that breaking point—the moment when regret and homesickness, and the urge to make things right, overcame any possible transgressions on her part—seem fated. The Australian looks down at the glossy pallor of her face. With tremulous fingers, he brushes damp hair from her forehead. Watching her dip in and out of something more leaden than sleep, his mind buzzes with questions about her relationship to Lock Jones. The answers he generated all those years ago now strike him as absurd in their unlikelihood, yet final nonetheless.

Deedee joins the Australian, who still kneels beside his mother. Margaret has begun to wheeze with each breath—not the dry harmonica chords of an asthmatic, but a rich, wet melody. Her sweat smells like rust. Every so often, her eyelids flutter open. Panicked outcries burst from her white lips: "Can't you understand—the baby cannot be left alone?" "Don't you dare start the funeral without me!" "Fetch my lipstick. I don't want to look like a dead person." "Am I late? Did I miss the whole show?" "Oh, dear. Oh, dear me." With each utterance, she is dragged further into the thick forest of her suffocation. Then she must claw her way back out, through coughs and gasps, before she can speak again.

The Australian stays with her, his heart racing, riding her death like a roaring wave. Deedee's eyes are closed and she is reciting a mantra in a strange tongue. The humidifier sputters in the corner of the room, but neither the Australian nor Deedee gets up to refill the water tank, and the night air is hot and dry. The long moments between Margaret's raspy declarations take on a cutting sense of immediacy, an ability to command his senses completely. Soon it is impossible for the Australian to bring into focus anything other than the bitterness of the roof of his mouth, his burning eyes, the flickering of the yellow lamplight, and the eeriness of Deedee's chants. Watching his mother struggle into death simplifies his existence radically. He is released from any sense of the past or future, untethered from himself and his life, enveloped in a peace that feels all wrong. Margaret's words become infrequent and incomprehensible, reactions to hallucinations. The silences between them grow longer, until finally only her wheezing is audible. Deedee takes hold of the Australian's hand. She weaves her fingers through his, and together they place their hands on Margaret's nightdress, over her heart.

"I love you so much," says Deedee. "I'll see you in the light." She leans over and kisses Margaret's waxy cheek.

Aware that his chance to say something to his mother will soon be gone, a shrill hum sounds from somewhere deep inside the Australian's skull. The hum winds through every vein and artery, shimmers down neurons and seeps through membranes, and finally encircles his eardrums so that he can scarcely hear. Nothing he wants to say is the sort of thing one says to a dying mother. "Did you know where Lock Jones was when I was growing up?" he wants to ask. "Did Lock know about me? Did you ever send the letter?" And, "Why did you leave it on the table, where I could see it? Did you want me to ask you about it? Why didn't I? Why was I so cowardly?" And then, "How sorry should I be? What should I regret most? How can I be a better man?" And, "May I have another chance at this, your death—and another chance with Fiona and Maximus?" And finally, "When will death find me? How, and at what age? How old will Maximus be when I go? And will he feel like this?" But none of this matters, not now.

The distance between each of Margaret's shallow breaths lengthens. The Australian must say something to her, quickly.

"She's leaving us," says Deedee.

Margaret exhales, groaning out a whole lifetime into the stuffiness of the bedroom.

"I'm sorry," says the Australian, unsure whether he is now speaking to Margaret lying in her bed or to no one at all. "Thank you, Mum."

"There she goes," says Deedee, smiling through tears. "Can you feel that?"

The Australian looks down at his mother's face, like the beach of some windless paradise. He feels a piece of himself, an internal knot or clasp holding him together—something he had taken for granted so fully that he'd never been aware of its existence—come undone.

Within a small storefront space, over whose doorway a sign reads TEMPLE OF SERENITY, the Australian sits beside Deedee as his mother's life is celebrated. It also happens to be Christmas Day. The room—which usually functions as a community center, art gallery, and meditation space—is filled with two dozen people, all dressed in bright summer clothing. A low stage juts at the front of the room, decorated with vases filled with red and purple flowers and a red clay urn containing Margaret's ashes. Everyone sits crossed-legged on the floor facing the stage. According to Deedee, Margaret requested that her funeral be joyous, an occasion for her loved ones to commune with her spirit through art.

Yesterday, Deedee suggested to the Australian that he participate, but he declined, citing his inability to perform any sort of creative act.

"Oh, that's OK," Deedee said. "Just speak a few words. You know what's in your heart."

Panicked at the thought of simultaneously embarrassing himself and besmirching his mother's memory, he repeated his refusal.

One by one, people mount the stage and pay tribute to his mother. An ancient-looking woman produces a long series of birdcalls, guttural throat noises and clicking of her tongue. A young Polynesian woman reads a poem about the orchestration of the ocean's tides by a musical moon. A tall, gangly couple sits with their legs dangling off the edge of the stage, singing and playing acoustic guitars—an original song called "Please, Please, Artemis"—while their grubby-looking ten-year-old son accompanies them on a plastic recorder. Next, a man who has brought a portable stereo does a psychedelic dance to techno music, involving the swiveling and blurring of his hands looping and tracing shapes in the air while the rest of his body remains absolutely still. A man who looks like a member of a motor-cycle gang reads a second poem, this one about the smoothing of a jagged mountain peak by the wind over time.

The whole thing is like a very weird talent show, a phenomenon the Australian is familiar with from television. As he sits cross-legged on the wood floor, pain radiates from his tailbone. His mother's death has taken on the quality of an overheard anecdote or outdated news story. The meaning of the word *death* is somehow too remote to speculate on. He attempts to recall his mother's role in important events from his past—her presence on the sidelines of the playing field when his cricket team won their division, her sympathy when his secondary school girlfriend ditched him for a university lad, her long embrace at Melbourne Airport just before he boarded a plane to America—but the memories slip away. In the face of the funeral's festive atmosphere, it is impossible to mourn simply and sincerely. He thinks of Lock Jones sitting behind the wheel of his pickup, and of his tiny teardrops, crystalline orbs affixed to his cheeks by surface tension. Margaret's words come back to him: "You are brave, like your father." The comparison shames him a second time.

It is not until Deedee mounts the stage that the Australian realizes she is no longer sitting beside him.

"I want to thank you all," she says, standing straight-backed in the spotlight. "Thank you, on behalf of Margaret, for your love and beauty.

You have honored her in the way she wanted, the way only her dearest friends could. Margaret had a deep love for Australia and its people. As many of you know, she went on frequent journeys to Aboriginal landmarks, to be quiet and present with rock formations, trees, the sky, and other sacred sites. Margaret knew that, according to Aboriginal tradition, each of these places has its own song. During her last few years, the time during which I was so very blessed to know her, she was working on memorizing those songs. It was her goal to spend a year singing her way along the Dreaming Tracks, the paths made by these sacred places, from the sea to the furthest reaches of the Outback. She wanted to do it alone, carried not by vehicle or strength of will, but by the power and love of spirits. And while she never had the chance during her lifetime, I am standing here—both as a medium, and as someone who loved Margaret deeply—to tell you that, through this celebration, we have released her soul, not to wander, but to focus on that very special journey. Friends, I can say with certainty that she is now gliding along those paths through which the greatest and oldest sprits flow. It is among their ranks that Margaret belongs, and in the songs that guide Australia's spirits."

As Deedee continues, the twenty-odd people filling the room nod with recognition upon hearing the facts of Margaret's life, but for the Australian, all of the information is new. He did not know, for example, that his mother worked in an organic food co-op and belonged to a community vegetable garden. He didn't know that she finally overcame her hydrophobia and learned to swim as an adult, that she volunteered at a battered women's shelter in a ghetto in Dandenong, that she developed shingles ten years ago and had suffered excruciating nerve damage in one side of her face ever since without even the slightest complaint. His mother was much stronger than he had ever given her credit for, a person of real substance. So much of what the Australian had thought of as flakiness had enabled her to inspire and elevate those around her.

Margaret's beneficence was not unlike Fiona's unconditional devotion to the pop star. So many people in the pop star's life view her as little more than a novelty and a cash cow. The Australian himself often dismissed her on those very counts. Fiona, however, has always seen humanity in the pop star, and in that humanity, intrinsic worth. He wonders why he exhibited so little respect for Fiona's generosity. The inconsistency of his devotion—his own flakiness—now seems a fatal flaw. And why had he possessed so little respect for Fiona's acceptance of *him*? She had stood beside him so patiently during his years of searching, the prolonged adolescence that he could never seem to shake. For the Australian, the question now is not how Fiona could leave him, but how she endured him for so long.

Grief has wedged itself between each of the Australian's ribs. Deedee finishes her eulogy and the room fills with jubilant applause. A clear image of his mother comes—Margaret walking alone along the Dreaming Tracks, not as a spirit but as the living woman he hardly knew. The Australian joins her, standing by her side in the shadeless expanse of the desert. Together, they look out at the horizon, where waves of heat like streams of molten, precious metals blur the distinction between land and sky.

Two days after the funeral, the Australian and Deedee must attend to the practical matters of Margaret's death. Margaret had been an only child. Her father died of an aneurism when the Australian was a boy, and after her mother's death a handful of years ago she was left with a significant inheritance. The amount slightly exceeded what she had spent in order to supplement her spotty income through several rent increases, and to support Deedee, who worked only occasionally for a house-cleaning service. When Margaret had fallen ill, she allotted a portion of her money to pay for her own cremation and funeral expenses, leaving just over eight thousand dollars behind.

That night, the Australian stands on the sidewalk. Fiona has not called him to offer condolences and comfort, which feels like a betrayal despite his failure to notify her of Margaret's death. He pulls his cell phone from his pocket and looks at the black screen. What is the purpose of calling Fiona? He is in possession of no relevant information so far as she is concerned. She never knew his mother and has little idea what Margaret meant to him. He cannot separate the fact of his mother's death from its significance, which is both too amorphous and colossal to communicate. Yet, according to some arbitrary social code the Australian finds despicable, he must call Fiona. Probably, he should have done so already.

Her phone rings twice before she answers. "I've been wondering if I'd hear from you," she says. "Is everything okay?"

Before the Australian can speak, the pop star's voice rises in the background. "Ha! Well, isn't that rich," she says. "This is exactly why I decided never to go to anything anymore."

"One sec," says Fiona in a low voice. "I'm really sorry."

"Fiona, have you seen the TV?" says the pop star. "They gave it to that Midwestern nymphet, the one who can't sing a fucking note. I told you it was a pity nomination. Didn't I tell you they'd never let me win? You'd think I'd died from menopause, how they treat me."

"Totally ridiculous," says Fiona.

"That vapid—that goddamn *fetus* gets best music video."

"They're idiots," says Fiona. "Why don't you turn off the TV?"

"Don't tell me what to do."

"This is an important call, actually. Let's talk about this in a few minutes, all right?"

"Everyone thinks they can boss me around now." The pop star is shouting. "Don't think I don't know how you all see me. Don't think—"

"Ten minutes," says Fiona.

The pop star mutters something unintelligible. The Australian hears footsteps as Fiona walks to another room.

"I'm so sorry about that," she says to the Australian. "I'm alone now. How are you?"

"My mum's gone," he says. "Three days ago. Some type of blood cancer, from what I can piece together. I'm still here, about to help sort through her things."

"This is terrible, sweetheart." She pauses. "Sorry, I didn't mean to say sweetheart. I'm just trying to say I'm heartbroken for you. This must be devastating."

The Australian is silent. Across the street, a pretzel vendor is closing the umbrella over his stand.

"Are you—well, of course you're not okay. I don't know what I'm trying to ask. Is there anything I can do?"

Fiona could fly to Melbourne. She could hold him, her arms wrapped around his waist, and press her face against his chest. She could ask him questions about his mother, and he could tell her all of the things he previously withheld, good and bad, and they could love Margaret together, share the pain, maybe get drunk. They could laugh at Deedee, something the Australian has no inclination to do on his own, but surely he would if Fiona were there and he could see Deedee through Fiona's eyes.

"Are you still there?" asks Fiona.

"Yes."

"Can I help in any way? I want to talk later. I can't tell you how sorry I am for your loss and for my—" she begins to whisper, "—situation right now. Maximus and I are living here, at the brownstone. It's just impossible."

"Of course," says the Australian. "I'll call you."

"Please do. And please know I won't stop thinking about you. And Maximus misses you terribly. And when you come back, stay with us here at the brownstone. The apartment is—I can't explain right now."

"I'll call you later," he says, and turns off his phone.

The pretzel vendor is wheeling his cart down the street. Two men tumble out the door of a pub next door, arms linked and laughing. They lean against each other, weaving their way around the corner. Heat lightning gilds the clouds lime green. The Australian has no intention of calling Fiona again. He waits for a storm to break. He wants to stand all night on the street outside the apartment, drenched and perfectly still. Every passerby will think him mad. He imagines an elegant woman shielding her hair with a newspaper, flitting her eyes toward him with bewilderment. He will stay in that spot until the storm passes. When eventually the clouds recede and the rain stops, he will not gaze upward at the stars. He will not seek the comfort of indoors. Exhausted as he is, he will not lean against a building. The night's heat will dry his clothes and hair, and he will experience a rebirth of some indeterminate kind. It will not be a relief. There won't be grace or hope. There will just be a difference, one that he cannot predict.

He waits. Lightning strikes again and again. But the rain never comes.

———

The Australian and Deedee sort through Margaret's belongings. All of her books, kitchenware, and clothes are set aside for donation to thrift stores, aside from those Deedee wants to keep for herself. She also retains Margaret's jewelry, cookbooks, artwork made by their friends, and mementos from Margaret's various travels throughout Australia and New Zealand—seashells and driftwood, two didgeridoos, shoeboxes of photographs, a small silk bag filled with red desert sand, and two vials of lanolin. Margaret never made a will, but Deedee declares with confidence Margaret's wishes for each object, invariably asserting that she herself is the intended inheritor. Although Margaret's true intentions are unknowable, the Australian tells himself he hasn't any right to feel disturbed by Deedee's presumptions. His role in the last long stretch of his mother's life was negligible. Furthermore, he has neither practical use nor any real desire for her things.

Soon he will return to New York City, where he intends to convince Fiona to take him back. No apology or explanation can undo his shortcomings, but maybe she will accept his current circumstances— the soul-ripping loss he has just endured—as adequate retribution. Perhaps she will feel bad for him ,enough to abandon the pop star. He must convince her to move back into the apartment with him, and from that close proximity he will win her over. Exactly how is yet to be determined, but his best chance will be a sincere show of humility and willingness to change. A more concrete plan will present itself—once the plane touches ground in New York, say, or when he sees Fiona's face. Meanwhile, he stands by while Deedee claims nearly everything for herself, breaking occasionally while she bicycles to available rental apartments nearby, looking for a place she can afford on her own. Two days before the Australian is set to leave, she finds a studio just a few blocks away. By the end of the following day, and with the use of a neighbor's van, the apartment—aside from Aphrodite and her cage—is entirely emptied.

After several hours of cleaning, the Australian stands sweating in the kitchen while Deedee sweeps the floor. As she drags the broom across the tiles, she wipes tears from her eyes, refusing his offers to take over. When she finishes, she turns on the faucet and gulps directly from the tap.

"Well," says the Australian, running an index finger through the dust on a windowsill. "I suppose we're done."

His duffel and knapsack are packed. With the physical reality of his mother's life cleared away, her presence in the apartment is gone. Without the sensation that Margaret might at any moment return, his attunement to Deedee is heightened—the razor-edged scent of her tea tree deodorant, her atonal humming, and the slight whistle when she breathes, presumably caused by a deviated septum. He has no reason to linger. He will hide away in a cheap hotel near the airport for his last night in Melbourne. He mops the sweat from his forehead with a sheet of brown paper towel. The trashcan is already gone. He balls up the paper towel and tosses it into the sink.

"Yes," says Deedee. "All that's left is the chest in the basement."

The Australian can recall no previous mention of a basement or any chest, and is peeved by the additional task. "All right," he says. "Let's have a look."

He follows Deedee out of the apartment and down a flight of rickety stairs, descending into what once must have been the cellar, back when the house was occupied by a single, well-to-do family. The basement is dank and, when Deedee shuts the door behind them, completely dark.

"I sense that you are burned out," she says. "It's understandable. I appreciate your help. The chest is too heavy for me to move on my own."

The Australian feels her radiating heat beside him, where she stands unmoving in the blackness.

"It means so much to me that you are lending a hand," she adds, her voice wavering slightly. "It must be an awful strain."

"No worries," says the Australian. "Let's get this thing moved."

The basement fills with harsh yellow light—Deedee has flicked on a switch—and the Australian quickly appraises the clutter of the building's tenants: an upended box spring, a lopsided couch, books, a few milk crates filled with records, a bicycle, plastic storage bins stuffed with clothing, and other domestic refuse. It is only when Deedee begins weaving her way through the scattered debris that the Australian's eyes land on the chest, its peeling peach-colored paint half-hidden beneath a dusty bed sheet. The chest is instantly familiar to him as the container of his mother's most private possessions. During his childhood and adolescence, she kept it locked, always. While he was growing up, on occasions when he was home alone and the idea came to him, he searched unsuccessfully for the key. He sees that the same bulky padlock is still fastened through its clasp.

"It's heavy," says Deedee. "We can drag it up the stairs, to the front stoop. I'll call a friend with a car to help me haul it over to my new place."

The Australian turns to face her. Feeling his trapezius muscles involuntarily stiffen with rage, he says, "No."

Deedee tries to convince him that her inheritance of the chest is predestined, and the Australian seethes. What begins as a brusque back and forth about their rights to it—son versus lover—soon becomes a full-blown argument.

"It is clear that you have no idea what's in it," says the Australian. "If my mother wanted you to have it, wouldn't she have told you what's inside?"

"You don't know what's in it either," says Deedee.

"This isn't right," he says, shaking his head and marching past her toward the chest.

Finding the chest much heavier than he expected, he struggles it across the cluttered basement. He has no idea where he will take it, or by what means it will be transported, but these things do not concern him.

He has nearly reached the door when Deedee cries out, "Wait!"

The Australian cannot steel himself against her. He sets the chest on the dirty cement floor and turns around.

"I didn't want to have to tell you this," she says, her eyes wild. "But Margaret's spirit guide came to me this morning, while I was in a state of half-sleep. She hovered over my bed—an angel. I felt the breeze from her wings fluttering in the air above me. 'The chest,' she said. 'The chest.' She said it again. How can we disrespect that kind of sign?"

Whether Deedee is being deliberately manipulative or is in fact mentally unwell cannot be discerned. The Australian tries in vain to reject his sympathy for her, the sense that she deserves his compassion—for the depth of her loss, certainly, if not for a chemical imbalance of the brain.

"Look," he says softly. "We don't even know what we're fighting for here. Do you know where the key is?"

"No," says Deedee, her voice thin and high, like a child on the verge of a tantrum.

"Okay," he says. "I'm going to run out for a moment. You stay in the apartment. I'll be back."

He walks Deedee upstairs, fetches his wallet from his backpack, and leaves her crouched by the birdcage, whispering to Aphrodite.

The Australian obtains directions to a hardware shop from a man selling bouquets of dyed carnations down the block. Fifteen minutes later, he returns to the flat with a hammer. Deedee follows him back down to the basement. The wood of the chest has warped and softened over the years, and it is an easy job, using the hammer's claw to pry off the metal plate to which the lock is affixed. When it falls to the floor with a clang, Deedee gasps. With some difficulty, the Australian raises the heavy and arched lid, its hinges thick with rust.

The contents are divided into three layers with folded bed sheets in between. On top are twenty or so old, glass soft drink bottles, stuffed with dried wildflowers: violet-colored waxlip orchids, which the Australian recognizes from his childhood visits to his grandparents' beach house in Geelong, as well as another purple flower, this one darker and formed by roundish puffs and some green and yellow buds. The flowers have crumbled with age, and when he lifts the bottles—Cascade and Passiona and Coca-Cola—from their bed of bunched-up newspaper, flower dust stirs inside them. The layer below is made up of ten or twelve file folders, unlabeled, each containing stacks of envelopes fastened into thick bunches with rubber bands. Beneath them, rocks ranging in size from lychees to persimmons line the bottom of the chest. It is as though Margaret wished to ground it in the event of a tornado, or to ensure that were a flood of biblical scale to swallow Melbourne, the chest would sink swiftly into a murky oblivion.

The Australian and Deedee both reach for the file folders. Sitting side by side on the gritty floor, they begin to examine the stacks of envelopes tucked inside each one. The first bunch of letters the Australian flips through is a collection of handwritten correspondence signed by Margaret's girlhood friend Sheila. They date back to Margaret's teenage years—the envelopes are addressed to her at boarding school—and the Australian is vaguely charmed by the bubbly handwriting and the youthfulness that the letters convey. "The suburbs are the stupidest compromise of modern life," writes Sheila. "They are supposed to be the best of two worlds—the city and the country. But they are the worst! We've got to get out!" In another, postmarked a couple of weeks later, Sheila writes: "I'm so sorry, Margie. Denis Becker held my hand and I didn't make him stop. I feel like the worst friend in the world, but I'd had a splash of wine. I know you'd hoped to be his girlfriend when you come home this summer. I'm through with him, I swear. I will do anything to make this right. Can you ever forgive me?" Margaret must have forgiven her, because the writing continues on for several years.

Deedee sits close beside him on the ground, flipping through letters written by a different hand. Her expression is tight, restricted. Glancing over Deedee's shoulder, he sees the chicken-scratch writing of a man, the lines of text bearing the slant and smudge of a left-handed author. The Australian, himself a lefty, is unnerved. He thinks of his father, and of the possibility of correspondence between Lock and Margaret. But how could that be, when Lock was illiterate?

As Deedee shuffles through the letters, her ability to hide her emotion weakens page by page, until she is plainly broken. When she sets the stack aside, moving dazedly on to the next, the Australian picks them up. Starting at the top of the first sheet, he scans downward until his eyes land on the closing, smeared across the bottom of the page: "Yours, Lock." The Australian flips back to the envelope, expecting the return address to specify some unpronounceable village in Southeast Asia or South America or Africa, or maybe Lock Jones's homestead—a dusty and desolate town in New South Wales. Instead, carefully printed on the envelope's upper lefthand corner is an address in Yamba.

While indeed located in New South Wales, Yamba is hardly the shantytown from which he has always assumed his father hailed. The Australian once read an article in an American travel magazine that ranked Yamba as the number-one most underrated vacation destination in Australia. The article's author described the town as "a sleepy seaside hamlet" and "a fishing gem," praising it for embodying "the mystique of the understated and undiscovered." The Australian remembers the accompanying photographs: a lush green golf course, surfers riding waves, and the silhouette of a couple holding hands, walking on the beach against the ecstatic backdrop of a rising sun. Without a word, he takes the stack of his father's letters upstairs, leaving the increasingly despondent-looking Deedee rummaging through the chest.

In the apartment, the Australian shoves the letters in his knapsack. Like a man trying to sprint along the ocean floor, he moves from room to room, remembering his mother in each one. For a few minutes he peers into the bedroom where she died. Bed, night tables, plants, geode, and humidifier—all of it gone. Collecting his bags, it occurs to him that he will likely never see Deedee again. Tenderness overtakes him, far beyond what he believes she deserves. When he returns to the basement to bid her goodbye, Deedee is still sitting on the ground with her head resting on the edge of the open chest.

"Deedee," says the Australian loudly, an attempt to rouse her.

She says nothing. He thinks she may have lost her wits completely. She murmurs something.

"Pardon?" he says.

She turns her head and their eyes meet. "She never told me about writing him. Nothing about him." She laughs bitterly. "I thought we shared everything, and I never even knew."

She turns her back to him, and then emits a terrible sound, half choke, half sob. Retreating, the Australian hesitates in the doorframe, but continues on. As he ascends the stairs, Aphrodite calls out from the apartment: "Love ya!"

He steps out into the heat-rippled city. When the front door of the old house shuts behind him, he becomes oriented to the trip ahead of him. Less than twenty-four hours later, he is deposited by Jetstar Airlines in Ballina. An hour after that, he is in a rental car rolling toward the end of a residential street, just inland from Yamba's idyllic Pippi Beach—a pristine curl of white sand and rock shelves wrapped around a turquoise curve of Pacific Ocean. Moments later, he is standing in front of the house from which his father's letters were sent.

PART FOUR

THE AUSTRALIAN PUSHES THE electronic doorbell. On the plane, he had read his father's letters, in which he pressed Margaret to allow him to visit her and the Australian in Melbourne. Lock had written that he had no money to send, and that his parents—who, in accordance with Margaret's bidding, had no knowledge of the Australian—weren't willing to give him any on account of his previous escapades. Margaret must have deflected him from her life again and again. Lock's acquiescence to her refusals demanded explanation. He could have found the Australian in the schoolyard after the last bell rang, swept him up in a hug and swung him in a circle. He could have shown up at the apartment, and if Margaret had tried to shut him out, he could have lodged his arm between the door and the frame, demanding to see him son. Or years later, when the Australian was in New York, Lock could have come to him, explaining man to man what—for all the years that mattered most—had kept him away.

The Australian rings the doorbell again. When a woman answers—sun-leathered, unsmiling, straddling the border between elderly and ancient—he realizes that, against all reason, he had hoped his father would be standing on the other side of that door.

"Yes?" says the woman. She is dressed tidily, in mint-green pants and a white button-down shirt with the sleeves rolled up. Her coarse gray hair is cropped short and immobilized by hairspray. She speaks with a broad Aussie accent, thicker than the Australian's. "Can I help you?"

He explains his predicament clumsily: that his father may have once lived in the house, and that he is in search of anyone who knew him.

The woman does not release her grip on the doorknob. "You must have the wrong address," she says. "This house has belonged to the same family since it was built. The Joneses—they own the Yamba Golf and Racquet Club. I've worked for them for thirty years."

Inside the front door of the ranch-style home, a sitting room with white shag carpeting and angular modern furniture expands beyond his view on the right, while a cream-colored grand piano is partially visible on the left.

"Sorry," says the woman, beginning to close the door.

The Australian puts a hand on the doorframe. "My father's name was Lock Jones."

The door halts, slightly ajar. A bird noisily shakes free from its perch in a bush beside the Australian and takes flight.

"Wait here," says the woman, flatly. She shuts the door completely, leaving him standing under the hot sun.

Rows of red, orange, and yellow flowers line a slate footpath that cuts through the green yard, ending at the sidewalk. The Australian takes a few steps back and a double carport containing a gleaming maroon Audi comes into view. From there, a driveway extends to the road. A mailbox is located at that junction—it is clean and white, with a miniature golf club affixed to its side, raised to indicate outgoing mail. The door opens again, and the woman is back, smiling now.

"Please," she says, waving toward the house's interior. "Come in."

The Australian follows her into the living room. He steps gently on the carpet, as though afraid of making a sound.

"Make yourself at home," she says, indicating a beige sectional couch shaped like a kidney bean. She turns away and vanishes around a corner.

The Australian sits on the edge of the firm couch cushion. Several minutes pass. It seems impossible that his father, the very same Lock Jones from Margaret's stories, had grown up here. There is the flush of a distant toilet, then footsteps. A man is walking through the hallways toward the living room. He is a head shorter than the Australian, wearing a short-sleeved white polo shirt and loose-fitting khaki shorts. The skinniness of his arms and legs is contradicted by his torso, which suggests, gently, the shape of a Bartlett pear. He has the sort of face—clean-shaven, bright blue eyes, few wrinkles—that, particularly when combined with total baldness, as is the case with him, makes age impossible to guess. As the man slips off his loafers at the room's edge and walks across the shag carpet, the Australian stands, wondering whether he ought to take off his own shoes. Before he can ask, the man is shaking his hand.

"Cameron," he says. "But everyone calls me Cam."

The Australian feels a queasy kind of letdown, once again, at the fact that this man cannot be his father. Cam sits down in the olive-green, pod-like chair under a bay window that looks out onto the lawn. As he leans back, he is enveloped by the chair, like a baby bird who, having deemed the world inhospitable, is attempting to reenter its egg. The Australian reclaims his place on the couch.

"I'm your father's younger brother," says Cam. "The resemblance is wild."

"I look like my father?" asks the Australian.

"Yeah," Cam replies.

Cam's hazy, adolescent demeanor takes the Australian aback. His lightly crow-footed eyes are bloodshot. The Australian explains the circumstances of his visit—his bewilderment over his interaction with the lawyer after Lock's death, the mystery of how she had located him, his mother's death, and his subsequent discovery of Lock's letters.

"The letters," says Cam, shifting in his seat and adjusting his shorts cuffs with a tug.

The Australian hears the rush of blood swooshing inside his head. "I was surprised because my mother had always said Lock was illiterate."

A branch of a flowering cassia tree scrapes lightly against the window, its yellow blossoms shaking in the ocean breeze. Cam narrows his eyes. It dawns on the Australian that his uncle is very stoned.

"Lock was brilliant," says Cam. "Beyond clever, but totally illiterate. See, he had severe dyslexia. Our father wanted to send him to a special school in Brisbane, but he ran away."

This statement is followed by silence during which Cam's thoughts manifest themselves on his face, but he makes no effort to communicate them verbally.

"Why did he run away?" asks the Australian.

"He didn't want to deal," says Cam. "Boarding school, all that." He explains that the family didn't hear from Lock for years, not until he joined the Royal Air Force. "He got discharged for going MIA during a training mission over Tasmania. He landed in a field and was discovered naked and wading in a bay, eating oysters and what have you. After that, we lost contact with him again."

"My mother told me a few details of my father's past," says the Australian. "Skydiving, mountain climbing, BASE jumping. Was he doing all those things during that time period—after he was discharged from the Air Force?"

Cam's focus drifts to some faraway place. "Some of them," he says. "Yes."

"When did you finally see him again?"

"Three years after he was kicked out of the Air Force. He showed up at the front door, here. He'd contracted malaria while knocking about South Africa in an anti-rhinoceros-poaching militia. There were loads of complications from the malaria, and he rested at home for two years. At that time I myself was out of commission. I weighed thirty-seven stone, mate. I was bedridden. Kaye—you just met her at the door—she took care of me."

"How did you lose the weight?"

"Right after our mum died, when I was twenty-three, I had my surgery—stomach staples. The weight fell right off."

"Good on you," says the Australian. "I'm sorry about your mum, though."

"Yeah," says Cam, with the stereotypical sincerity that is particular to the intoxicated. "Pancreatic cancer. After we lost Mum, Dad was never the same. He finally joined her a few years ago. A series of strokes over the course of a few months."

"My condolences," says the Australian.

He hopes the conversation will now veer back to Lock Jones and the letters, but Cam continues to spout off. After he lost weight, he was reborn—a new man with fresh ambition. He attended the

University of Sydney, where he earned a degree in mathematics. His marks were high, and he even contributed to an important break-through in applied statistics, but upon graduation he chose to honor his father's wish that he return home to manage the affairs of the family business: the Yamba Golf and Racquet Club. He did this out of gratitude to his family, who had supported him during his convalescence, and so that his father could retire.

The Australian nods periodically, seething at his uncle's meandering. It seems a miracle when the conversation finally returns to Lock.

"About your father," says Cam, sending a jolt through the Australian.

"Yes?"

Cam leans forward in his chair and rests his forearms on his sinewy thighs. "While he was recovering, he swore me to absolute secrecy. Then he told me about your mother, and you. He asked me to write those letters. He spoke the words and I transcribed them."

"Did he every talk about me? Beyond the letters?"

"He was too private for that," says Cam. "Not just about you. He wasn't a verbose fellow."

The Australian inquires about the inheritance bestowed upon him by Lock.

"My best guess is that it was the money our mum left to him," says Cam. "I never knew what he'd done with it. Quite honestly, I assumed he'd frittered it away."

The Australian tells him the amount, and the year in which he received it.

"Yes, that's exactly right. He must have saved it all that time, for you."

This notion softens the Australian, but those feelings are quickly eclipsed by anger at the fact that there were gifts much more valuable than money that Lock had withheld. "Why do you think my mum told Lock about me, when she had no intention of allowing us ever to meet? Do you know?"

"I've always wondered the same thing, mate," says Cam. "I know she was dead set on raising you alone."

"But why?"

"Let me think," says Cam. He closes his eyes, pinching the bridge of his nose between his thumb and index finger. Time flows around and through the Australian. Just as he begins to wonder whether Cam has fallen asleep, his eyes snap open.

"In one of her letters, she mentioned something about the Divine Feminine," he says. "Also she had this idea that, biologically, the next evolutionary step for humankind will be women's ability to procreate without any outside genetic input."

Some distant moment in the Australian's own childhood in which Margaret said something similar sparks, and then fades into ash. "Oh," he says, quietly. "She didn't say anything else?"

"I'm sorry," says Cam, shrugging. "I don't remember all that much."

He narrows his eyes and scrunches his forehead. "All I can add," he says, "is that your mother was cool. *Too* cool, if you know what I mean. Maybe part of her did want you to know Lock, but it was like she'd made some kind of vow. Like, extreme self-sufficiency. Something about her parents. She wanted to do it all on her own—to succeed at that."

This explanation, however dissatisfying, resonates. The Australian wants to fight against it, to will into being a history less damning of his mother. Yet her particular brand of pride seems a truth carved deeply into stone, traced and retraced by each year he knew her.

"My brother respected her," Cam says. "He wouldn't just pop up at her doorstep. He wanted to win her over with the letters. I told him to make a move, she has no right to keep you from your son, but he wouldn't."

"Why not? Didn't he want to know me?" The Australian is surprised both at the rawness of his wound and the fact that he has revealed it so plainly.

"You've got to believe me," says Cam. "Lock cared. Letter after letter, Margaret put up barricades. It turned him inside out. He grieved for not knowing you, but he wouldn't cross her. Their time together was brief, but I'm sure that he was deeply in love with her."

Cam looks at his watch and announces he is expected at Yamba Golf and Racquet. "Want to come along? Check out the club?"

"Sure," says the Australian, unsure what another option might be.

Behind the wheel of his car, Cam slips into a cheerful persona, one more befitting the owner of a beach town country club. Cruising slowly down his tree-lined street, he explains that despite its name the club no longer houses any racquetball facilities.

"A few years back, I had the courts ripped out and turned that building into a social hall. Sometimes we host events—wedding parties, retirement bashes, and the like. Otherwise, it's used for live entertainment on Sunday nights. We've been able to snag some good ones."

"Oh?" says the Australian.

The ocean appears out the window. As the car glides along parallel to the coastline, he imagines himself out there, at twenty years old—half boy, half Poseidon—paddling out on his surfboard into the open sea. He pictures his hands cupped into powerful shovels, hurling great curls of water behind him, churning waves upon the waves.

They roll past the club's sign onto a narrow drive, which winds alongside the club's eighteen-hole golf course.

"Have you ever heard of Lily Blundell?" asks Cam. "I've got a meeting with her and our event staff now. She's a musician, one with a very famous sister."

"Can't say I have," says the Australian.

"Well, certainly you've heard of Celeste."

"Yes, of course." The Australian is still thinking about the sea, longing to be alone on that empty beach. If he were there, perhaps he could cry, which is all he wants to do.

"Lily Blundell is Celeste's younger sister," says Cam.

"Is she really?" The meaning of Cam's words snaps into focus. When the Australian was in university, Celeste had been named Australia's sexiest woman by the Australian magazine *Stargaze*. Just that morning, on a television at the airport, he watched her speak out against a common practice in the fashion industry in which designers give models clothing from runway shows in lieu of cash payment. A retired supermodel, she is now spokeswoman for several human rights organizations whose fundraising campaign ads are internationally televised. Most of all, the Australian is familiar with her because of her ongoing feud with the pop star.

The feud began nearly fifteen years ago at a British awards ceremony, when the pop star presented Celeste with a special achievement award for her Nourish the Youth campaign, for which Celeste had spent eight months in the Sudan filming a documentary called *Only*

Hope. According to Fiona, Celeste—having just been handed her golden trophy—thanked the pop star by the wrong name. She quickly and gracefully corrected the error, but she then proceeded to repeat the mistake in conversation with a celebrity gossip columnist at the award show's afterparty, and then again when confronted by the pop star on the red carpet of another event a few weeks later. Celeste sent the pop star an apologetic note and lavish bouquet of flowers. This did little in the pop star's opinion, to set things right.

Over the years, whenever the two women have bumped into each other at benefits or other industry functions, the pop star has snubbed Celeste. What's more, ever since her own career has been in decline, the pop star has underhandedly trashed Celeste to the press. "Poor thing," she once said, shaking her head with theatrical dismay during an interview on an internationally syndicated talk show. "We all have our struggles. But trichotillomania—the compulsion to pull out one's own eyelashes—how painful and grotesque. I just pray she gets the help she so desperately needs." Celeste, whose lack of eyelashes since birth is well documented and much celebrated by her admirers, has consistently risen above these smear tactics, declining to respond when asked for comment.

Cam parks the car in front of the clubhouse and pulls his key from the ignition. "There's a rumor going around," he says, turning to the Australian. "I can't promise anything, but there's a chance Celeste will come to the show tomorrow."

Before his meeting, Cam leads the Australian on a tour of the country club. Given the flashy modernity of Cam's house, the club is surprisingly quaint and outdated. It is late afternoon, and the grounds are deserted aside from a few leisurely golfers dotting the course's distant sprawl. Inside the clubhouse there is a small pub and a low-ceilinged dining hall in which the waitstaff, wearing a uniform of forest green polo shirts and khaki pants, are busy laying down table-cloths in preparation for dinner. Cam proudly points out a menu posted on the wall by the hostesses' station, and the Australian sur-veys its offerings: two buttery preparations of local prawns, fried and bread-crumbed King Island Brie, chili chicken wings, pepper-crusted Nolan grain-fed eye fillet served with a parmesan béchamel sauce, breaded veal scallopine, and several other dishes, all of them over-wrought. Fare this heavy, this overburdened by sheer number of in-gredients and quantity of grease, hasn't been in fashion in New York, or the major Australian cities for that matter, since the 1980s. As soon as the Australian thinks this, he feels the urge to smack himself for being such a snoot.

He thinks of Fiona, who has always adhered mostly to a vegetar-ian diet yet inflicts no judgment on others. While she would never prepare meat for the Australian—in part because she preferred not to handle it, but also because he did most of the cooking—there was a time when she delighted in his enjoyment of a good steak, particu-larly one prepared in the Argentinian style. That was his favorite meal at Ignacio's, one of the few restaurants for which Fiona could ever find time, given the demands of her work schedule. Located just two blocks from their apartment, the restaurant was convenient and also happened to be very good.

Following Cam through the clubhouse, past golf trophy display cases and sweaters with the club's crest sewn onto their breasts, arms outstretched and nailed to the wall for display, the Australian tries to recall the last time he and Fiona ate at Ignacio's and cannot. Instead, he remembers one of the first times, an August evening during a heat wave, just weeks before Maximus's birth. They sat in a corner by the window, beneath the cool blast of a central air-conditioning vent, holding hands at the center of the table. After they had finished their meals, Fiona drank the remainder of her mint-lavender iced tea while the Australian used the crayons provided in a scotch glass on the table to sketch nude depictions of himself and his wife, eight months pregnant, on the white paper tablecloth.

As he did so, he took inspiration from Albrecht Dürer's famous engraving, *Adam and Eve*, which he had recently seen on a solitary trip to the Metropolitan Museum of Art. Struggling to mimic the soft yet precise shapeliness of Eve's form, he found himself adding folds and rolls of flesh to Fiona until her torso resembled the body of an elongated Shar-Pei. Then, as he fashioned his own musculature, his attempt to echo Dürer's athletic Adam begat a jagged and robotic monstrosity—abdomen, thighs, and biceps forming in accordance with the geometry of nightmares. By the time he finished the double portrait, both he and Fiona were laughing to the point of tears.

The Australian follows Cam outside, across a narrow courtyard, and into the building that once housed racquetball courts, which is now called Sinclair Hall in honor of Cam and Lock's late father. Inside that cavernous space, stage lights glow dimly from the high ceiling, just barely illuminating the dark wood paneling on the lower third of the walls. The center of the room is filled with small round tables, each set with white tablecloths and two chairs. Jutting from the back wall is a wooden stage. On the left is a bar occupied by a small cluster of employees, along with a woman in her mid-forties with a feathered haircut, wearing high-wasted denim shorts and a tight, white T-shirt. Cam waves at the group and together they wave back, except for the woman, who is examining her cuticles.

"Lily! Friends! Sorry for the wait," Cam shouts. "Must run off now," he tells the Australian, slapping his shoulder. "Go back to the clubhouse, mate. Kick back. Have a drink, or three."

The Australian returns to the pub. He feels none of the pride, disappointment, visceral familiarity that he assumed would come to him by connecting with his father's roots—only the same longing for something other than the cold distance he always felt whenever he looked the photograph of his father. He sits on a stool at the middle of the empty bar. The two weeks he has spent in Australia feel like ages: decades away from Fiona and Maximus, centuries witnessing his mother's death, and millennia seeking out elusive truths about his father. Today is his birthday. Having decided to drink himself into apathy or blindness, whichever comes first, he asks the bartender for the club's signature drink, whatever it might be.

A Lemon Ruski—lemonade and vodka—is set down on a napkin before him. He remembers drinking grapefruit shandies with Fiona on the evening they first met. "Shut up," he mumbles. The bartender glances at him. The Australian lifts his drink to his lips. Two sips in, he is seized by the hot, tight embrace of nausea. Hoping the chill of the beverage will be soothing, he takes a big gulp. The back of his tongue burns with stomach acid.

Abandoning his cocktail, he steps quickly out into the courtyard. It is 6 p.m. and dry heat radiates from the yellow disc of the sun, still high in the cloudless sky. He leans over behind a bush, hands on his thighs, and takes a series of deep breathes. Minutes pass—two, three, four. Confident now that he won't vomit, he drags a wooden deck chair to the edge of the courtyard, where the shade of a golden ash tree blooms against the cement, and collapses into it. Soft breeze stirs around him and he closes his eyes. A weight sets into his bones.

The Australian thinks of Maximus in the fragmented way that occurs during half-sleep, a colorful montage of associations. Moments with his son, on which he has been afraid to dwell for fear of heartbreak, resurface. One by one, they rush to the barricade he erected upon leaving New York, flowing through every crack and gap.

There is Maximus, emerging from the bathroom after peeing all by himself and in the general direction of his training potty, beaming with satisfaction. There is his laughter, like a cluster of tiny bubbles escaping from a slim fissure in the ocean floor—rising, rising, free. There is his plump little hand, warm and perpetually sticky, gripping the Australian's index finger with impossible, beautiful force. There he is fast asleep, dreams fluttering behind his milky eyelids—and between his parted lips, a teensy orb of saliva expanding and contracting with each long breath, glittering in the glint of his dragonfly night-light. There he is at the neighborhood playground, giving away his toys to any child who shows interest in them, until, empty-handed and alone, he watches, quiet and content, as a girl collects pebbles in his bucket, a boy digs with his shovel, and another girl runs sand through his blue plastic sieve into the large, loose pockets of her dress. The memories keep coming, each sharp-edged fragment of love penetrating deeper, slicing through the Australian until he buckles into an agitated slumber.

When he is woken by Cam, with a startling shake of the shoulder, the sun is sinking toward the crown of a hill on the golf course, the sky a cobalt blue. Club members have begun to arrive for dinner, shuffling awkwardly past the Australian before entering the clubhouse. Cam invites him to spend the night at his home. Having reached the end of his own ideas about anything, the Australian lamely accepts.

On the drive, he struggles to keep his eyes open. "I just need a nap," he says, pressing his forehead against the cool glass of the car window.

Cam glances at him, his expression vaguely worried. "No problem," he says, and turns on the radio.

For the rest of the ride, Cam taps his fingers on the steering wheel to the beat of a song by the pop star, one the Australian once secretly liked and which he hasn't heard in years.

At the house, Cam asks Kaye to show the Australian to the guest bedroom. She smiles, revealing tea-stained teeth, the same yellow-brown as a cockle's shell.

"This way," she says, walking brusquely down a hallway.

The Australian follows. Earlier that day, when he first arrived, he dropped his duffel bag in the house's entryway. Having long since forgotten about it, he is grateful to find it resting beside a dresser in the small bedroom.

"Can I bring you anything?" asks Kaye. "A glass of water? An extra fan?"

"No, thank you," he says.

He sits on the edge of the bed, unties his shoelaces, removes his trainers, and begins to knead his sore feet. It seems impossible that Lock Jones spent his childhood in this house. Cam, with his confidence in running his father's country club and comfort living in the family home, must be a typical Jones. Could the same ever have been said of Lock? Or had he always been different? The Australian chooses to believe the latter. Lock had been bold, challenged his parents, shot like a bullet from Yamba. The Australian looks up and is surprised to see Kaye still in the doorway, leaning against its frame. She is scrutinizing him so intently that she seems not to realize he has noticed her watching him. Then she appears to catch herself and erupts with a smoker's laugh.

"Ay," she says. "I don't mean to stare. It's just the resemblance. I'm sure Cam's told you already."

The Australian is silent.

"Right," she says, backing out into the hallway. "I'll rack off now. G'night."

The next morning, the Australian emerges after eleven hours of sleep to an overcast sky and a silent house. Wearing boxer shorts and a T-shirt, he wanders the hallways, peering into rooms until he is sure he is alone. A note from Cam is taped to the bathroom mirror, stating that he will return at 5 p.m. to take the Australian to Lily Blundell's show at the club. In the kitchen, the Australian locates a cordless phone resting in its cradle on the wall beside the refrigerator. Outside the kitchen's panoramic window, rain begins to fall.

The Australian's calling card is in the guest room, but certainly Cam owes him an international phone call at the very least. He dials the United States country code, followed by Finn's cell phone number. The phone rings once, and then again.

"Hello?" Finn's voice comes through the line over the whirr of street sounds.

"It's me," the Australian says.

"Brother!" says Finn. "How the hell are you?"

"I'm in a nightmare. It's been a rough time, mate. I can't get into it now. Please, I want to know how you are. What's new?"

"Are you sure you're OK?" asks Finn. It is clear that news of the Australian's separation from Fiona has not yet reached him.

"I'm surviving," he says. "I'll give you the rundown later. I just need you to tell me about yourself. Please."

"Well, a lot's happened since you left," says Finn. "Work is basically over for me." He explains that the pop star called into a morning radio show, hosted by a notorious shock-jock, to announce her retirement and declare herself a recluse. "She doesn't need me anymore. The timing is perfect, though. I'm going to open my own salon. Figuring out how to back it, the money, that's where I'm at."

"Brilliant," says the Australian, doing his best to sound enthusiastic. "It's about time."

"We'll see," says Finn. "I hope so. But that's not the big news around here."

"Tell me the big news."

"OK, here goes," he says, taking a deep breath. "Something incredible happened to Vivian and I. This is going to sound insane, but we were sledding in Central Park and we met this couple, Michelle and Laurent. She's a graphic novelist and he's a high school guidance counselor."

"OK," says the Australian.

"They're polyamorous," Finn continues. "Just like Vivian. They love who they love—each other and whoever else. And actually, it's awesome."

"All right." The Australian is wary of where Finn's story is heading, yet wishes he were hearing it across a table at a café.

"I could never wrap my head around Vivian's whole poly thing," says Finn. "You know that. But everything changed when we met Michelle and Laurent. Vivian and I—we both really hit it off with them." He clears his throat. "What I'm trying to say is, we fell in love."

"What do you mean?" asks the Australian.

"We all fell in love with each other," says Finn. "I just opened up, you know? It's not just that I'm into Michelle, who by the way is gorgeous and wonderful. You'll adore her. It's Laurent and I, too. And Michelle and Vivian. There's this electricity—this perfect connection between all of us. It's beyond anything I could have imagined."

"Wow." The Australian clears his throat.

"I know this must seem ridiculous—it all happened so quickly—but we're getting married. Not legally, obviously. It'll be a commitment ceremony."

"All of you, together?"

Outside the kitchen windows, the rain begins to fall in sheets.

"Yes," says Finn. "In May."

Finn's situation strikes the Australian as familiar in its absurdity, which calms something inside him. However, that effect quickly dissipates. As his friend carries on about his burgeoning four-way romance, the Australian's conception of their New York life skews. From this new angle, his and Finn's lives appear chaotic in the most banal sense of the word, little more than the result of a series of random impulses, flurries of spasm and twitch. His own life is a meaningless anarchy. The idea that anything worthwhile is waiting for him—a life of his own, aside from Fiona and Maximus, or even the seed of one—is a delusion.

Finn segues to Vivian's film career. *Visions of You* has won Best Screenplay and Best Director at a small but well-regarded film festival, garnering her the attention of important people within the industry.

"Fantastic," says the Australian. "Please give Vivian my congratulations."

After hanging up with Finn, the Australian calls Fiona. Outside, the rain has powered up into a rolling, booming storm. Leaning against the kitchen island, phone pressed to his ear, each ring is met by a desperate refrain emitted from deep inside him: *I need her, I need her, I need her.*

Fiona's voice comes through a web of static: "Jesus. Why are you calling me from an Australian number? I thought you were back in the city."

"If I were back," he says, "I would be there."

"Well, clearly." Her voice has a hard edge, even through the wall of fuzzy reception.

"I mean I'd be there, with you," he says, immediately regretting it. Before Fiona has the chance to take pity—to soften her voice and remind him that their marriage is over—he asks to speak with Maximus.

"That's fine," she says. "Hold on."

The implication of her words—*that's fine*—spreads and multiplies like a virus, infecting the Australian's every cell. The suggestion seems to be that it is somehow generous of her to allow him to communicate with his own son. Perhaps she has undergone a drastic change during his absence—she may have turned against him completely. This new Fiona might regard him much as his mother regarded Lock Jones.

The Australian's mother never had any grasp on the practical, had offered no guidance in matters that—during his youth, and to this day—seem fundamental. He had learned so much of the necessary repertoire of boyhood through trial and error: how to roller skate, how to shave, how to swing a cricket bat, how to pick out cologne that girls would like. There were skills he never learned, which perhaps a good father could have imparted: how to hold down a job, how to laugh at himself, how to render a proper apology, how to be quiet and still without a profound sense of dread. An image comes to the Australian of his son, alone and shivering in a field whose tall, yellowed grasses are etched with sparkling frost. His skin tightens with panic and rage.

"Daddy?" Maximus's gentle voice is barely audible through the crackle of the bad connection.

"Darling," says the Australian. "How's my little lad?"

"Daddy?"

"Yes, love—it's me. I miss you like crazy."

"Daddy?" says Maximus. "Daddy?"

"Can you hear me?" asks the Australian. "Are you there?" Thunder booms nearby. "Hello? Maximus?"

There is a long pause, and then Fiona's voice comes through, barely intelligible. "We can't hear you. The connection is horrible. Sorry."

"Fiona." The Australian is shouting into the receiver. "Can you hear me now? Fiona?"

The line crackles loudly and then goes dead.

The Australian thinks of Roper Thomas, a classmate of his from secondary school. The two of them had been friendly, but not quite friends. Three weeks before graduation, Roper killed himself by injecting air into a vein using his diabetic grandmother's insulin syringe. As the storm gradually decelerates to a drizzle, an image of him visits the Australian. He had never thought much about the suicide before—he never accepted that ending one's own life was a thing that could be done—but now the event returns to him, and he wonders why it happened.

Roper was a good-natured prankster, a bassist in an unremarkable garage band, and a benchwarmer on the football squad. His marks were average, his parents happily married, his family middle class. The only thing that set him apart was that, although he wasn't particularly attractive, he was extraordinarily popular with girls. He was attentive and compassionate in a way that none of the other boys were. He took genuine interest in comments girls made in class and remarked upon them later. He seemed to be able to morph into different versions of himself depending on girls' desires—yearnings that perhaps the girls themselves were unaware of until he managed, in a thoughtful word or two, to fulfill them completely. Yet he seemed undistracted by thoughts of romantic conquest.

While some of the other boys suspected Roper was gay, he maintained his popularity with them. Between sports and barbies and house parties, he affirmed and empathized with them, too, in ways so subtle as to never fracture the boys' pride. In the Australian's own moment of weakness following the breakup with his girlfriend, Shanna, Roper—although they had spoken very little during the preceding three years of their acquaintance—provided him with advice that the Australian recollects as being paternal and providing him with particular solace. While he can't recall Roper's exact words, he can remember that in the bathroom where Roper had discovered him, weeping and pissing at the same time, the Australian had felt carried. Not like a child in his caretaker's arms, but like a wounded soldier slung over a sturdy shoulder. Afterward, the painful emotions remained, but he trusted that help was on the way, that relief was imminent. Aside from party banter and shouts across a football field, it was the only conversation they'd ever had.

The rain has stopped. The Australian collapses into a chair at the breakfast table, rests his forehead on the glass tabletop. Roper's motive for suicide comes into focus: he had no respite from the burden of his own empathy. His seeming ordinariness must have been an attempt at self-protection, a sort of camouflage. A way to avoid being targeted by other boys for being soft, attacks he could not have weathered, and also to hide from those looking to unburden themselves. Still, there was no preventing the people around him their suffering. Sensing his compassion, they sought him out. Cutting those people off would have required either callousness or indifference, neither of which Roper possessed.

He was unable to turn away. He inhaled every sorrow, cloaked himself in every joy, and shed none of it. Yes, he had essentially been killed by the generosity of his spirit. The day he died must have been the day he reached maximum capacity.

All of it seems so clear to the Australian. It is also seems obvious to him why Roper chose the method he did—silent and literally sterile. A hypodermic needle would leave no visible mark, no open wound through which his loved ones might enter him and thereby come into contact with the great storehouses of anguish within. Why had Roper chosen air over poison? Unlike cyanide or bleach or morphine, air is nothing at all.

The Australian takes a cold shower. Back in the guest bedroom, the idea of unzipping his duffel bag and assembling a new outfit is daunting. He slips on yesterday's pants and shirt. Only once he is wearing them does he notice their rankness. Back in the kitchen, he is tempted to lie down, spiraled like an embryo on the little turquoise rug in front of the oven. Why he does or doesn't do anything, everything for which he feels an inclination—the alien logic behind his restraint—is the greatest mystery of his life. It seems entirely possible that had he heeded every instinct from the day he was born, he would have been better off.

If only he had relied solely on his natural impulses, they might have become exquisitely refined; or, alternatively, they might have expanded into tools of great power, both destructive and creative, swollen into monstrous density like the muscles of a mythical beast. Animal intuition, sharper hearing, quickened heartbeat, a taste for raw and gristly meat, and total ignorance of cultural and moral conventions—maybe these are the things he is missing, the losses incurred by the atrophy of his primitive brain centers. Living in the civilized world has been his undoing. The Australian wonders whether he is losing it or finding it, and he wonders what is meant by *it*, this thing that seems to be absolutely essential to everyone's existence, which no one dares to name.

He has not eaten since his arrival in Yamba. In the refrigerator there is a large plate of corned beef and smashed potatoes covered with plastic wrap. A small note from Kaye rests on top of it, explaining that she prepared the food for dinner the previous night, and that while Sunday is her day off, she thought he might like a nice hot lunch. He could put the food in the microwave, but a warm meal will only depress him more. He scarfs down the cold food without enjoyment. Then he returns to the guest room, lies on the bed, and reaches for the leather sleeve containing his passport and the photograph of his father. The sleeve had been a gift from Fiona years ago, when they still planned to travel together. Between his fingers, the leather feels stiff and waxy. He returns the sleeve to the table and spends the next several hours flipping through a stack of twenty-year-old *Australian Geographic Outdoor* magazines from a wicker basket by his bedside.

Cam picks up the Australian and takes him to Yamba Golf and Racquet. During the drive, the Australian again stares out the window at the white-capped sea. Cam has been talking for the entire ride, but the Australian doesn't tune into the conversation until they are already halfway to the club.

"She's been boozing all bloody afternoon," he is saying. His face is red and his knuckles bloodless on the steering wheel. "She's never done this before. She's always been very professional. I've known her six months and I'm telling you, this isn't the real Lily."

"Oh," says the Australian.

"I told her to please go easy," says Cam. "There's the show tonight, of course. But more importantly, I feel responsible for her."

"Why?"

"She wasn't doing well when I first hired her," he says. "She'd been living in the middle of nowhere with some chap. A boy, really. Just barely eighteen. I'm pretty sure he was stealing from her, whatever money Celeste was sending. One of my employees knew Lily—his brother was once in a band with her. He urged me to invite her to audition, said she needed a fresh start. She's very good. I hired her on the spot. Anyway, before I came to fetch you, I asked her if she's upset because her older sister is coming to town. Lily denied it, swore it had nothing to do with Celeste. I'm certain, though, that's got to be it."

"It must be very difficult to have a sister like Celeste," says the Australian.

"Exactly," says Cam, punctuating his speech with a slap to the steering wheel. "Now, don't get me wrong. Lily is a fine musician. She's the best we've had. But let's face it—it's a gig at a country club. Her sister is Celeste, man. *Celeste.*"

"Right," says the Australian, only now truly appreciating the reality of Celeste's imminent appearance.

"When I found her, Lily lived in a yurt with a bloke who calls himself The Real Deal." Cam shoots the Australian a meaningful glance.

"Jesus." The Australian is awash in a noxious sort of sympathy. Lily's disaster is a reminder of his own—Cam's pity mirroring what he believes his friends, if he let them in on the truth, would feel for him. He dreads meeting her and wonders if there is a way to avoid it.

"It's a bad situation," says Cam. "As we speak, she's probably still at the bar knocking back Singapore slings."

"Can't you call it off?" asks the Australian.

"No way. According to Lily, Celeste is en route to Yamba. She just wants to come support her sister, but Lily can't see that. Tonight will be rough—it's going to be one hell of a bodgy show—but we'll get her though it. You and me, pal."

"We will," says the Australian, intending to inflect it like a question but somehow neglecting to do so.

"That's the ticket." Cam grips the Australian's shoulder with his faintly liver-spotted hand. "We'll make this work."

In Sinclair Hall, the forty-odd club members, hunched around circular tables with tea candles at their centers, are speaking very little to one another, and those who are speaking are whispering. The space hums as though in the aftermath of an event of high significance, one capable of disorienting and enervating people. The Australian assumes it has to do with Lily. Perhaps she has made an outrageous scene or a dramatic exit.

The barman—stout and in his twenties, a bush of red hair flaming around his paper-white face—is staring with eagle-like intensity toward the back of the room. There, in the shadows, is the silhouette of a tall, broad-shouldered figure.

"Where is Lily?" Cam asks.

"In the ladies'," replies the barman. "She's been there since just after you left."

He nods toward the dark table in the back, where the figure is seated, and Cam's eyes follow.

"Fuck all," says Cam. "Is that *her*?"

"Yes."

"Why is there no drink on her table? Is she being taken care of?"

"Of course," says the barman. "She didn't want anything." He shrugs.

The Australian understands that the figure is, indeed, Celeste. His eyes gradually adjust to the dim lighting. She is reading a book spread open on her table.

"Come on." Cam tugs on the Australian's shirtsleeve.

Approaching Celeste's table, the Australian sees the title printed on the book's spine—a biography of the famed primatologist Jane Goodall. When Cam and the Australian are standing directly before her, she removes from her lap a tasseled bookmark, places it in between pages, and looks up. Breathlessly, Cam introduces himself to Celeste and welcomes her to the club. "Thank you," she says, standing to shake his hand. She smiles and nods at the Australian, whom Cam seems to have forgotten completely.

Many models the Australian has encountered in his New York life have, up close, looked—with their spindly limbs, oversized heads, and wide-set eyes—like beings from outer space. This is not true of Celeste. Having retired from fashion modeling well over a decade ago, she has become zaftig. At six foot three, she is a powerful presence in such a way that is inspiring, regal. Her chestnut-brown hair is shorn close to her scalp, revealing the perfect curvature of her skull and allowing the gold flecks dancing in her deep brown eyes to dominate the impression she leaves.

"Is there anything I can get for you?" Cam asks, gesturing toward the bar. "A drink? Something to eat?"

"I'm quite fine," she says. "If you could please just let my sister know that I'm here, that would be fabulous."

"Of course. We will tell her straightaway." Cam bows, a quick tip at the waist, and the Australian follows him—like a dog, he thinks—to the ladies' room.

After calling out into the lavatory to make sure it isn't otherwise unoccupied, Cam enters and the Australian follows. Beneath the last stall door, two red cowboy boots are visible.

"Lily, dear," says Cam, his voice thin with caution. "Are you all right?"

"Is she here?" Lily asks, slurring.

"Yes," says Cam. "She is very excited to see you."

"Do you know what happened last time we were together?"

"No, I can't say I do."

"It was two years ago," she says. "We had a blowout."

"I'm sorry to hear that," says Cam.

"Don't be sorry," Lily snaps. "I'm not sorry. I'm not sorry about a bloody thing. She tried to trick me into ditching the love of my life."

"The Real Deal?" asks the Australian. The words launch from him by some automatic mechanism, similar to the one that induces a sneeze.

"Yeah," says Lily, apparently unconcerned by a stranger's presence in the ladies' room, in possession of the details of her private life. "I told my sister to go to hell. I told her I loved him. I loved him so much. Oh God," she wails. "I love him still."

"You did the right thing, doll," says Cam. "You can do much better than that. You *will* do much better."

Although the Australian is invisible to Lily, he nods in earnest agreement.

"She made me doubt myself," Lily says, sobbing now. "I should have said no to you, Cam. I don't belong in Yamba. I shouldn't have left him to come here. Oh, God." She blows her nose loudly. "She put it in my head that my life was all wrong. I heard her. I listened. I believed her."

This isn't the Australian's mess. He has trouble enough for a hundred people waiting for him in New York. Indeed, it is ridiculous that he has become ensnared in this fiasco—and for what? Cam has been no help at all. The Australian will now thank him for his hospitality, hitchhike back to the house, retrieve his rental car, and drive it straight to the airport. But in the instant that he opens his mouth to say so, the stall door swings open, so quickly that the two men must jump aside in order to avoid being hit.

"Fellows!" says Lily, beaming.

Though her features are coarser than her sister's, the Australian can see her resemblance to Celeste in her Roman nose and brown eyes flecked with gold. She twirls away, tosses her snotty tissue into the toilet, and turns back to them. Once again Cam has failed to introduce him.

"I'm ready," she says, holding her arms out theatrically. Her eyes are rimmed only slightly with a faint pinkness.

"Are you sure?" asks Cam. "You're feeling well enough?"

"You know what?" says Lily, still a bit slurry but far more chipper. "I've never felt better in my life. I feel clean—*cleansed*, really. I needed that. Oh boy, did I need that."

Moments later, Lily takes the stage, gripping her acoustic guitar by its neck. Cam leads the Australian to the end of the bar. Club members reposition their chairs in order to ensure a good view of the entertainment. Lily stumbles but manages to mask it by falling into the wooden chair at stage center, as if that had been her intention precisely. She clears her throat and scans the crowd. Her roving eyes land on her sister.

"I'm going to play a song for you," she says into the microphone. "Thanks for coming out tonight," she says, slowly strumming her guitar. "I'll start with something old."

In the first few bars, the Australian recognizes a folk song that he knows from ages ago, perhaps a favorite of some long-forgotten, musically inclined boyfriend of his mother's.

"Oh come along," sings Lily, so close to the microphone that her lips brush against it, which causes her husky voice to be overly amplified, "all you sailor boys and listen to my plea. And when I am finished you'll agree—I was the *goddamned fool* in the port of Liverpool." She narrows her eyes into an accusatory stare.

"Bugger," Cam says under his breath.

The Australian is allied with Lily—she is as much of a mess as he feels. Watching is like witnessing the unfolding of his own disaster.

"Oh," she continues, "I started drinking gin and was neatly taken in by a little girl they all called Maggie May." Her voice becomes gruff and very loud. She whips her head from side to side like an angry lion. "Oh Maggie, Maggie May," she belts, appearing on the verge of tears once again. "They have taken you away to *slave* upon that cold Van Diemen shore! Oh, you robbed so many sailors and dosed so many whalers, you'll never cruise down Lime Street anymore."

Celeste is sitting tall in the back of the room, but her expression is obscured by darkness. Lily is nearing the end of the song and has worked herself up into the sort of condition for which an exorcist might be summoned. "Oh, Maggie—Maggie May," she roars. The club members sit motionless, neglecting their cocktails. The Australian can feel the heat of their stares, the burn of their judgment and the sting of their pity. Lily strums the final chord, hard and slow. She lets it reverberate into the ghastly purity of the silence that follows. The Australian is shrinking, mortified.

Then comes the applause. It is startling and thunderous, much louder than the number of people in the room could possibly generate. There are hoots and hollers, and here and there people rise from their chairs, clapping their hands in the air above their heads. "Brilliant," someone says. "She is *hilarious*," says another. "What a card." The club members have interpreted the performance as some kind of gag. When the applause dies down, they begin to sip their drinks and chat amongst themselves. On stage, Lily looks out across the banquet hall, wearing an expression of naked astonishment. Beside the Australian, Cam sits on a barstool, his nostrils flaring and collapsing with each strenuous breath. In the back of the room, Celeste's chair is empty.

The Australian holds out for as long as he can, while Lily edges closer to total loss of control. The club members grow rowdy, possessed by the self-surprised raucousness of people who are usually reserved. Between the third and fourth songs, the Australian leaves the bar, slinks along the wall toward the exit, and bursts out the door into the twilit courtyard.

"Pardon," says a woman's voice. The Australian turns and finds himself face to face with Celeste. "You wouldn't happen to have a piece of nicotine gum, would you?"

The Australian pats his pockets despite the fact that he has never chewed a piece in his life. "Sorry."

"Oh, don't be sorry," she says. "I haven't chewed it in years. I shouldn't have even asked." She laughs, kicking the grass with the toe of her knee-high boot. "Quite a show in there, don't you think?"

The Australian casts his eyes down.

"I hate coming home—to Australia, I mean," she says. "No offense."

"None taken," he says. "Believe me."

"Say what you want about the States, but in New York they leave you alone. Less people know who I am there, of course, but it's a cultural difference as well. It's too much for me here. I try my best to avoid it."

The Australian responds with a single nod.

"From the minute I get on that plane, it's a nightmare," she continues. "I'm not complaining about being—well, anything, really. Don't think I am. My point is that I have no motive to be here anymore, other than my sister. I only ever come for her, and it just seems like she's doing everything she can to push me away."

"You're talking about Lily?" asks the Australian, because it seems like the polite thing to do. "She's quite talented."

"That's hardly relevant anymore," says Celeste. "She's a mess. I've tried every conceivable way to help her."

"She's lucky to have a sister who cares."

Celeste makes eye contact with him for the first time. "Do you have family?"

Perhaps because of Celeste's fame, or due to her frankness despite their strangeness to one another, the Australian immediately assumed her to be a narcissist of the type that will emote unabashedly, effusively, but will—in the very next moment—have no memory of the person to whom they have been confiding. He is familiar with this sort of person, via his connection to the pop star. But he has misjudged her. Beyond her distress at her reunion with Lily, there is kindness in her face. Beneath her sadness lies a firm bed of confidence—not self-importance or arrogance, but the sureness of a woman who trusts herself.

"Do I have family?" the Australian says, as though repeating her question aloud will make it any easier to answer. He could easily return to the fabrications he presented to his dying mother, but Celeste's honest and total way of listening releases something in him, and he unloads the whole truth. "Well, my wife has just left me. We have a son, Maximus—three and a half. I need to win them back, but I don't know how. They're in New York, where I still live, I guess, although I no longer have an apartment there. I'm almost broke and I've got no job prospects. Years ago I worked in finance, but I can't reenter that world—it's been too long. And aside from Fiona and Maximus, I suppose I don't have any family. I never knew my father, and he died years ago, anyway. Last week, my mother died, which was the reason I came back to Australia. After them, who's left? I'm an only child. I have an uncle, my father's brother, and I just met him for the first time, hoping he would help me learn about my father, but I'm nothing to him, and frankly he is nothing to me. So that's my situation."

The Australian marvels at his own boldness, which he is certain Celeste has inspired. Her presence will give him the strength to face any truth. He feels a strong desire for her to ask further questions, so that, in answering, he might finally know his own mind.

"I'm so sorry for your losses," she says. "And I apologize, by the way, for not asking your name earlier. Silly me—I assumed you worked for the club."

The Australian thanks her and introduces himself.

"Listen," she says. "I'm not much of a drinker, but I think we could both use one. Wouldn't you agree?"

The Australian and Celeste return to Sinclair Hall, ignoring the spectacle that continues on stage. They bring the drinks back to the courtyard and sit in side-by-side deck chairs still damp from the morning's rain. They discuss Celeste's struggles with her sister, and then, when prompted by the Australian, she describes her own family. Her husband, William, is a classical cellist—"a true cellist's cellist," she says. They have two sons: Atlas, fourteen, and Emmanuel, seventeen. She speaks of their life in New York, tucked away from the public eye in a SoHo loft—a tight-knit bunch, she explains, despite tension caused by her sons' eccentric teenage phases, the details of which she promises would bore the Australian to bits. "Tell me about Fiona," she says, and then takes a short pull of scotch through a red cocktail straw.

The Australian sips his pint. "She's the love of my life," he says. "Well, I know that's what everyone says. I met her at a bar in the East Village a few years after I moved to New York. I had a few bucks in my pocket but no idea what to do with myself. I probably would've had to leave the States. No Green Card, no job, no ideas."

"What is it that you love about her?" asks Celeste. "What is she like?"

"Well, for one thing," he says, "she's the mother of my child. And she is a wonderful person. She works for a very troubled woman, and she's incredibly patient with her. She's basically a saint. And with me—she has tolerated so much. All this time, I've been trying to figure out my life. Sure, she's leaving me now, but for years she put up with my confusion. I owe her everything."

An uncomfortable pause wedges itself into their conversation. The Australian downs the second half of his beer in one long chug. Celeste breaks the silence by inquiring about his Green Card status.

"Oh, I got it years ago," the Australian replies.

"That's remarkable," she says. "That business can be difficult enough, but without a job it's often impossible. Did that come through before or after you married Fiona?"

"After," he says. "It was incredibly lucky that it all came together like it did."

"Sounds like it," she says. "Very fortunate. How did you get by for so long without job, especially after your son came along?"

The Australian inspects his empty glass and then sets it on the armrest of his chair. "Like I said, I owe it all to Fiona. She's an angel. Above all, I love her for that—the goodness of her heart. I should have done more to show my gratitude. Without her, I don't know what would've become of me. I should have thanked her more, for everything."

Celeste, lit golden by the streetlamp beside them, appears lost in thought. The last rays of sunlight slide behind the dark slopes of the golf course. Night birds call out in the purple dusk.

"Here's the thing," she says. "And I hope you don't mind my saying this. But it seems to me that what you really owe her is an apology."

"Absolutely," the Australian says quickly. "You couldn't be more right." He shudders despite the warmth of the evening. "I need to apologize for not doing my part in the marriage. I've got to do something big to make things right."

"Not exactly," says Celeste. "This is only my perspective, and I don't even know you. But it sounds to me like what you really need to apologize for is convincing yourself you loved her, marrying her for a Green Card, and then letting her operate under the assumption that your feelings were genuine for so long."

"You don't know me—I love Fiona," he says, straightening his posture. "I love everything about her. I need her."

"Well, that's where I think you're right," says Celeste, gently. "You *need* her. Or at least, you believe you need her. Your union did result in a Green Card, correct? And she does support you financially, yes?"

Retorts swarm the Australian's mind, only to scatter and vanish like roaches in the sudden flash of a kitchen light.

"Well?" asks Celeste.

"Yes," he says, "but—"

"It's just—do you want to hear this?"

He thinks for a moment before nodding his affirmative.

"It seems that you can't tell me one thing about her aside from what she's done for you—nothing specific to her, nothing that only you know and love," says Celeste. "If you asked why I love William, I would tell you that he drinks four cups of Darjeeling tea per day, and sometimes I find him scrubbing a spoon while he's doing the dishes, furiously trying to clean off a tea stain. If he doesn't know I'm watching he will carry on and on, trying to polish a single spoon—and I will feel joy, because his attention to that spoon is so meticulous and deliberate, and those are some of the traits that made me fall in love with him almost twenty years ago. What I'm getting at here is that, from where I sit, your feelings seem to have very little to do with the reality of who Fiona is. It sounds like you wish to remain with her because, as you said, she saved you from yourself. Under the guise of romance, you essentially made of her a Green Card, an ATM machine, and a companion in a tough city." She uncrosses her arms and leans toward him. "Who is she? What is she like? You haven't told me yet."

"She is the mother of my child," says the Australian. He flips back through the years, searching. "She tells the most wonderful lies," he adds, although he can no longer remember a single one.

Celeste reaches across the gap between them and places her hand on his shoulder. His last defenses fall away, whipping and twirling into the distance like cornhusks on the wind.

"How do you know all this?" he asks.

"Don't take this the wrong way," she says, "but you're not as complicated as you think. No one is. Not really." She leans toward him, the golden flecks in her eyes accented by the yellow light of the streetlamp, her irises blooming like marigolds. Close enough to his ear that he can smell her cool, mineral fragrance—not a perfume, but her own natural scent—she says, in a whisper, "Not even me."

Celeste decides to leave Yamba Golf and Racquet and head straight to the airport. She bids the Australian farewell, handing him her phone number penned on a bar napkin, which he shoves in his pocket. "Let's grab a coffee sometime," she says.

The Australian's ability—his exceptional aptitude, really—for self-delusion sickens him. Why was he such a willing target for her forthrightness? And did her honesty unfurl to the point of abuse? No, her words had come from genuine concern—but if thrust with enough force, the blunt knife of a letter opener can be no less fatal than a switchblade. Why did she persist in exposing his selfishness, which now disturbs him to the point of derangement? Perhaps she harbored a mistaken notion for the potential of a more enlightened person hiding somewhere deep inside him. She must have conceived of her insights as tools with which he might chisel away at his defects. She mistook him for a better man, and he cannot hold it against her. Nonetheless, he can never face her again.

In his bank account, the Australian has just over three hundred dollars. With the purchase of a last-minute standby plane ticket to New York, a transaction made over the phone at the club, his credit card limit is exceeded. He can no longer justify an attempt to reunite with Fiona. To do so would only inflict further cruelty. And certainly he cannot take her money. Where he will go after his arrival at John F. Kennedy International Airport and how he will survive in the city are puzzles he will attempt to solve midair.

At ten thirty, the Australian and Cam return to the house. Cam sits on the living room couch smoking a bong while the Australian readies himself to leave. While packing his clothes in the guestroom, he grabs several *Australian Geographic Outdoor* magazines at random from the bin beside the bed and tosses them into his duffel.

As he finishes zipping shut his bag, Kaye appears in the doorway.

"Hitting the road?" she asks. "I don't blame you," she adds, before he can respond. She crosses her arms and leans against the doorframe. "I practically raised those boys. Sometimes I fault myself for how they ended up."

"No worries," says the Australian, slinging his knapsack over his shoulder.

"Wait a minute, would you?" she says. "I want to talk to you about your dad. That's why you came, and I can't let you leave with nothing. It's not right."

The Australian sits stiffly down on the edge of the bed. Kaye straightens her back, as if poised to make a public address.

"I'd worked for a few other families before I met the Joneses," she says. "I'd been around loads of children by then, knew all about the things that scared them. Monsters, thunderstorms, fever dreams—every little one has their fears. I always knew what to do about them, what to say. That went for Cam, too. He was an easy one. But your father was different. See, Lock was the most fearful child I've ever known. He was scared of just about everything. The feeling of wool against his skin made him scream bloody murder. The tiniest bit of rind left on an orange threw him into a fit. If it touched his teeth, he would be a blubbering mess. Even at the age of nine, if he looked out the window and saw a cat walking nearby, he would hide under his blanket for hours."

"My father?" asks the Australian.

"Oh, yes," says Kaye. "And he had night terrors. He was an incurable bedwetter. He was a fragile boy, which is why we were all so shocked when he ran away. We thought he'd been kidnapped. Nothing else made sense. It seemed impossible that a lad with his temperament would set out alone."

"Seems like everyone was wrong," says the Australian, angered both by Kaye and his own impulse to defend his father.

"Oh, I know the stories," she says. "Skydiving, fooling with wild animals, flying around in tiny planes, all of that nonsense. I know that's the version of the story you've heard, and I know what you must be thinking: If my father was so brave, why couldn't he face me? Why did he wait until he died to contact me? I couldn't help but overhear your talk with Cam. Believe me, I'm familiar with his version of things. But I've got to give you the Lord's honest truth. I don't know whether Lock loved your mother. But I do know what kept him away, whether he loved her or not."

"What is it that you believe?" says the Australian, making no effort to hide his bitterness.

"He was a boy so scared of life that he died trying to prove otherwise. But he didn't quite get it right. Life stuff never stopped spooking him, the real stuff—relations with his parents, his brother, *himself*. You were the most terrifying thing ever to happen to him. Like I've said, I knew him well, maybe better than anyone. He could wrestle a crocodile, but he could scarcely have a conversation with another human being. How he ever confided in me the times that he did, I don't know."

She pauses, staring for a moment at the ceiling, and then returns her attention to the Australian. "He created an idea of this man," she says. "Exciting, wild, brave. That was his gift to you, that legacy. I'm certain that's how he thought of it, that the idea of himself was better than any reality he could have offered."

"But what about the letters?" the Australian asks. "What you're saying isn't true. He tried, he wanted to be with me and my mum in Melbourne."

"Whatever he told Cam to write is one thing," says Kaye.

"What is your point?" asks the Australian.

"My point, honey," she says, "is that those letters don't tell the truth of Lock's heart. He may have loved your mother, and he may have wished he could be in your life. But the fact is, he chose to stay right here. I believe that if your mum would've had him, he still would have stayed here—sitting right there on that bed, the one you're sitting on now, crying to me, like he did so many times, that he just couldn't do it." She straightens from the doorframe and brushes some imaginary dust from her shirtfront. "I hope knowing that helps you," she says, her voice unsteady. "I really do."

In a daze, the Australian leaves Kaye and Cam to their strange little lives. Driving to the airport, he blasts the radio at the highest volume he can tolerate. He wants to cry, wishes he could. At the airport he collects his standby ticket. He expects to wait a long time, maybe even days, for a seat on a New York–bound flight, but he is able to board the very first one. Learning of this bit of good fortune ignites a sense of foreboding. This luck may represent the final installment of his ration, a precise amount that was allotted to him on the day of his birth and which has now all been parceled out.

Once in the air, he tries to sleep but cannot. He drinks gin and tonic while staring at the sunset over the silver arc of the oceanic horizon. On a monitor affixed to the seatback in front of him, he attempts to watch a subtitled German television show about people who raise orphaned baby animals on a farm in Bavaria, but he cannot concentrate. Leaning his head against the smudgy airplane window, he shuts his eyes.

Three thousand feet above the Earth, a portrait of Lock Jones assembles itself. By the time the plane is over Samoa, the Australian is confronted with a revised portrait of his father: a man whose childhood peculiarities grew malignant, who abandoned his son to a world that he himself was too cowardly to inhabit, instead barricading himself inside the safehouses of whimsy and paralysis and dreams, leaving his own future—and his son's—to fate. The Australian envisions Lock Jones as a lonely wayfarer wandering a white desert landscape in search of color, magic, and light, scouring great cities and ragged wilderness for any means of redemption, and finally looking upward, searching for a trap door in the sky. In that portrait, the Australian sees himself.

When the plane touches down in Hawaii for a two-hour layover, Kaye's sun-damaged visage comes back to him. He remembers her turning to leave the bedroom, and then looking back. "Being your dad was the greatest adventure Lock's life served up," she said. "And it was the only one he ever turned down."

PART FIVE

THE AUSTRALIAN STANDS IN front of his old building in New York, fumbling with cold-stiffened fingers through the pocket of his knapsack. His spring jacket offers little protection from the wind. At last, he fishes out his keys, lets himself in, and rides the elevator to the fifth floor. In the hallway, poised to unlock the apartment's front door, he hears a man's voice from inside, bellowing and too muffled to understand. A shrill woman's voice cuts in: "You deserve it, asshole! Admit it!" Both of them laugh uproariously.

The Australian knocks on the door, two sharp raps. It opens immediately. Before him stands a woman in her early twenties, gasping for air amidst all the hilarity. In hot pink shorts and a man's white undershirt over braless and surgically augmented breasts, she evokes the type of coed on spring break in Cancún or Daytona Beach or New Orleans during Mardi Gras who exposes herself to camcorder-wielding pornographers in exchange for a hat or some beads.

"Yeah?" she says.

He peers beyond her into the kitchen, still furnished with his and Fiona's table and chairs. A behemothic man—shirtless, near the Australian's own age, still chuckling—ignites the stove's gas burner, places a half-smoked cigar in his mouth, and bends down to the flame. He puffs a few times, filling the air with stink. Then he turns off the stove and leans lazily against the kitchen island.

The Australian explains that until recently he lived here.

"Oh my God," says the woman. "I love your accent."

"Did you buy this apartment?" he asks.

"No way." She dismisses the notion with a sweeping wave of her hand. "I wish I owned this place. I'm subletting. Did you not know that? That's crazy."

"How do you know Fiona?"

"I met her last year when I came to New York to dance for the video for '4ever True.'" The pop star's only work since her trip to South American and the onset of her affliction, the song remains memorable to the Australian—in it, the pop star's vocals are layered over the mating calls of Peruvian katydids. The song was supposed to result in the first of three Amazon-inspired music videos, altogether called *Holy Treenity,* but it fizzled out the minute it hit the airwaves. "My roommates dropped some major bullshit on me last week because I was, like, five minutes behind on rent," says the woman. "Anyway, I had nowhere to crash. I was going to have to go back to Reno, and I fucking hate Reno. Fiona is the best. This apartment is totally amazing, and way cheap."

"You two, just—enjoy it." The Australian backs away from the doorway, dizzy.

"Oh, there's no *you two.* Billy's just a friend." She turns toward the man, revealing the word YUMMY printed in baby blue letters on the seat of her shorts. "A brand-new friend. Right, Billy?"

Billy, who is picking flecks of tobacco from his outthrust tongue, nods in agreement.

She turns back to the Australian. "He doesn't live here," she says in a loud faux whisper. "Well, not yet!"

The pair explodes into another fit of laughter. Billy doubles over the kitchen island, coughing out billows of smoke, which flatten against the purple slate countertop like mist sliding across a field. The slate was harvested and honed in a cooperatively run quarry in Vermont—Fiona purchased it three years ago using her Christmas bonus from the pop star. The cigar smoke collides with a half-empty bottle of margarita mix, which forks its path.

From the street, the Australian calls Finn and learns that he and Vivian have begun cohabitating with Michelle and Laurent but are currently in Boston for the filming of Vivian's latest short film, *Across the Pond*. Partly inspired by the pop star, it depicts a long-distance love affair between an American sculptress with micropsia and an acerbic British art critic. Finn insists Michelle and Laurent would gladly host the Australian—they know all about him and are dying to make his acquaintance. Reluctantly, the Australian phones them. When no one answers, he hangs up on the machine. Calling Celeste is out of the question. An invitation to coffee is one thing. Asking to spend a few nights in her family's home would likely make her uncomfortable or even disgust her, and eliciting her distaste would be worse than sleeping in a park.

The Australian needs shelter—warmth and a place to think. He sets out for Esperanto, where he hasn't been in years. From Chelsea he walks south, still hauling his duffel bag and backpack, pushed by a stinging wind down the wide artery of Eighth Avenue. It is 9 p.m. on a clear-skied and freezing Friday night. In the Meatpacking District, the sidewalks swarm with people. Clubbers have yet to emerge, but hipsters, young bankers, and the night's first wave of the bridge-and-tunnel crowd convene outside bars and restaurants, smoking cigarettes or waiting for friends. In the West Village, a woman shouts profanities at no one from within the dark recess of a defunct phone booth. A group of teenagers shoves past the Australian, nearly knocking him to the pavement. Esperanto is a beacon, a spark in an endless night. Turning onto MacDougal Street, he is almost there. He will spend a few of his last dollars on a peppermint tea, warm himself before the flames of the other patrons' youth, and forget his life for an hour or two. Through that forgetting, clarity will come. He will know whom to call, where to go.

Halfway down the block, in front of the coffee shop's familiar brick building, he stops. Esperanto has been replaced by a fitness studio.

The weight of the Australian's luggage seems to quadruple. As though emboldened by his abjection, the wind blows harder and colder than before. Standing in the middle of the sidewalk, he is oblivious to the people brushing past him, cursing him for blocking their paths. Only now, standing inches from the storefront window of the fitness studio—Joan of Arc Boot Camp—does he appreciate that a night class is underway. Beneath fluorescent track lights ten women lunge, kick, and slash through the air with wooden staffs. Their movements are perfectly synchronized, a musical simulation of violence. They are lead by a woman with flaxen hair and a gymnast's body. The studio's doctrine, which is taped beside the window, states that the bootcamp will "awaken the warrior forces within any woman." The Australian scoffs.

As he watches the women, they meld into a single entity, like a galaxy viewed through a telescope from millions of light years away, whose luminous elements—hundreds of billions of stars, interstellar gasses, and cosmic dust—are visible as one scintillating gold-silver whorl. He is mesmerized for the remainder of the routine. The instant the women lay down their staffs, they become distinct. They are gregarious and shy, slender and fat, laughing and yawning, youthful and middle-aged, and one of them elderly. They are mopping sweat from their forehead with a bandana, crouching to remove a water bottle from a gym bag, leaning against the wall, stretching their hamstrings, gathering their hair in a barrette, shaking tension out of their muscles, falling back into formation. As they take up their staffs, the Australian admonishes himself for criticizing the studio's doctrine. Maybe this is exactly how Joan of Arc would wish to be commemorated—precisely the context in which she hoped to be invoked. Maybe this fitness studio is but one room in the endless palace of Joan of Arc's heaven.

The Australian shivers, hugging himself against the cold. Were he to ask any of these women if he might sleep on their couch, they would reject him with ease. They would not martyr themselves for nothing, and he is nothing to them. His hands and feet have lost all sensation. Unequipped for the elements, he has neither the street smarts nor the will to survive in the outdoors. He imagines himself dead on the sidewalk, curled with his head resting at a queer angle upon his knapsack, face coated in ice crystals that sparkle in the morning light. What could people say about him, other than that he died for nothing?

He reaches into his pocket and pulls out the napkin penned with Celeste's phone number. He will ask to stay with her and her family. Probably, she will say no. If she turns him away and he dies, it could at least be said of him that he tried, that all his life and until the end he tried—that he is the patron saint of trying.

———

The Australian's reawakening nerve endings burn. He sits on a buttercup-yellow velvet couch at the edge of a sparsely furnished loft. Celeste and her husband William occupy Victorian armchairs facing the Australian, to his left and right, respectively, with a royal blue divan between them. It is impossible to pinpoint the means by which she and William communicate their sublimity—it is simply their nature. The Australian dimly recalls thanking them for their hospitality, which Celeste extended to him on the phone for one night only. Again, he voices his appreciation.

"Not a problem," says William. In his early sixties and African American, he wears a Merlot-colored cashmere sweater and jeans. He lifts a thick pamphlet of logic puzzles from an end table beside his armchair. Seeming to have done so out of habit, he briefly considers its cover and sets it back on the table. Smiling at the Australian, he exudes the same self-assurance and openness as Celeste, who sits cross-legged, looking cozy in black stretch pants and a gauzy tunic made of some off-white natural fiber.

"We're glad we could help," she says.

"Asking for help is a difficult thing to do," says William. "There was a time in my life when I had to do the same."

"Oh?" says the Australian.

"At nineteen, I was awarded a full scholarship to study at Juilliard under my idol, the inimitable Miloš Dvorsky. Needless to say, I felt like I had arrived. But when I got to New York, I fell into some bad financial straits. I ended up staying with various classmates for a semester. I'll never forget it—asking all of these virtual strangers for help. It was the most difficult thing I'd had to do."

A bitter cackle surges up through the Australian's throat. His attempt to hold it in produces an amputated snort.

"The generosity of my classmates taught me something important," William continues. "Being a good person isn't enough. You have to give your heart a vehicle, live beyond your mind. You have to act."

Desperate to change the topic, the Australian asks whether their sons are home.

"Yes," says Celeste. "They're holed up in their rooms. We'll invite them to join us, if you'd like."

"That would be great," says the Australian.

Celeste and William exchange glances. Taking a cell phone from the end table, William punches out a text message, and there is a whoosh as it is sent.

Seconds later, the two boys emerge from side-by-side doorways at the far end of the loft and come sit together on the divan between their parents. William facilitates introductions.

"So, what's your deal?" Emmanuel looks pointedly at the Australian. Seventeen and handsome in the way that teenaged boys can be handsome when they have recently growth-spurted into burliness, he wears a T-shirt depicting a bald eagle in flight, gripping an outline of New York State in its talons. The Australian does not know how to answer. His hesitation seems to satisfy the boy, who crosses his arms over his broad chest and leans back on the divan. "Mom said you need a place to sleep tonight. Sounds like you're homeless."

"Manny, please," says Celeste.

"Well, isn't he? If he has a home, why isn't he sleeping in it?"

"Listen to Mom," says William.

The parents' pleas seem only to puff Emmanuel up.

"You got a job, bro?" he asks, leaning in toward the Australian.

Celeste straightens in her armchair, as though about to spring out of it, but she does not. "I'm telling you, nicely, to cool it."

The pain inflicted by Emmanuel's accusations is superseded by the shock the Australian feels at Celeste and William's inability to stand up to their son. They both look to the Australian, silently communicating a sheepish semi-apology: *We're so sorry*, but also, *You know how it is*. Meanwhile, Emmanuel reclines in a pose of exaggerated relaxation, smirking. Sitting silently beside him, Atlas, fourteen—small for his age and wearing a navy-blue jumpsuit with a NASA emblem on the left breast—never lifts his gaze from his lap.

"Are you on welfare?" Emmanuel asks. "Food stamps?"

"That is very inappropriate," says William. "If you don't tone it down, there will be consequences."

The Australian feels something akin to gratitude. Emmanuel's abuse of him has effectively commandeered the spotlight. Tonight, when everything seems contrived to enhance his failures, insults are welcome. They minify him, inspiring in him the pathetic hope that he might simply evanesce. "No worries," he says quietly. "He's just curious."

"I'm not curious," Emmanuel says. "I know exactly what's going on. The guy is looking for a handout. He's the problem with this country."

The Australian offers to leave, but Celeste puts up her hand.

"Absolutely not," she says. "Emmanuel, please go to your room."

Emmanuel shoots up from his seat. "You're Nazis," he says, making eye contact with each of the adults. "All of you."

As he marches away, Atlas rises from the divan and follows his brother.

"A bunch of freaking Hitlers," Emmanuel shouts from the far end of the loft. "What happened to freedom of speech? Have you ever heard of a little thing called the Constitution?"

He enters his bedroom and slams the door behind him—and, marching into the room beside his brother's, Atlas does the same.

The Australian lies on a leather futon folded out into a queen-sized bed in a corner that usually serves as Celeste's office. Everyone else has gone to sleep. The lights are off and the loft's many curtainless windows admit the city's glow, a cool blue that gels over everything. A chill wafts from a window near the Australian's head. He pulls a wool blanket up to his chin.

After the boys' departure, Celeste and William confided in the Australian their distress at Atlas's behavior, not Emmanuel's, whom they insist is simply going through a rebellious phase. They fret for Atlas because for the last seven months he has refused to eat anything besides astronaut food that he orders over the Internet from a wholesaler: freeze-dried ice cream, squeeze tubes of fruit and vegetable purées, cubes of dehydrated chicken and beef.

"We don't know what triggered this fixation," William said. "We don't know how to help him."

Atlas's obsession is worrisome indeed, but Emmanuel's aggression strikes the Australian as no less troubling. It is obvious that the boys' maladjustments stem from their parents' lack of backbone. Witnessing two sane and sophisticated people incapable of perceiving an obvious reality disconcerts the Australian profoundly.

Yet, beyond that, something else rises up in him: envy. Despite their dysfunction, or perhaps because of it, Celeste's family as a whole surpasses any fantasy the Australian has ever had about what a family could be. The four members are a unified entity, like an atonal melody whose discordant notes comprise a beautiful whole, or a thriving ecosystem constituted of perfectly balanced elements—flora and fauna, predators and prey—all of them cupped beneath a lush canopy of their knowledge that they belong.

The Australian sleeps lightly, waking again and again, peering out the window each time. The half moon is visible, then obscured by a tall building, then comes into view on the other side. The stars dim, fade out completely, and the sun begins to rise, the sky like the center of a halved, radioactive peach. Pigeons coo on a ledge outside the window. Having run out of clean clothing days ago, he puts on something from his duffel bag, wrinkled and smelly. In the shower-less bathroom Celeste assigned for his use, he splashes water on his face and brushes his teeth. The family is still sleeping. The Australian exits through an industrial metal door into the building's stairwell: exposed cinderblock walls and bare cement stairs leading up to the roof. At the top is a skylight.

He punches Fiona's number into his cell phone. He must see Maximus, today.

"You're back," she says. "Before you say anything—I feel completely awful about your mother. I'm so sorry, just incredibly sorry." Her words vibrate with the buzzing energy either of mustering the courage to voice them or of holding them in until now. "And I deeply regret how everything's been, all the crap that's happened with us. I never wanted things to turn out like this."

"Everything's all right," says the Australian.

"The connection died when we talked last time. I meant to tell you about subletting the apartment, but I heard that—well, you know now. That must have been a horrible shock."

"It's fine," says the Australian. "Really."

"Please, just listen. Can you hear me out for a minute?"

"Of course."

"I've been bogged down in my own bullshit, working nonstop, absorbed in my own world, and also the pain of what happened before you left. I didn't put enough thought into what you were going through in Melbourne. I was totally selfish. And now I'm doubting everything."

The Australian burns to exploit her faltering resolution to leave him. He wants to tell her that he is suffering too and that he wants another chance. But that would be cruel, his old self coming out to wreak havoc again on Fiona's present and, if she were to agree, her future.

"Give yourself a break," he says. "You're overthinking things."

"I regret you had to go through everything in Melbourne alone."

"I'm just glad I made it. I should have been there for my mum all along."

"You couldn't, though," says Fiona. "You were here, with us. You were doing your best."

"My best is a fucking zero," he says. "I've messed up everything."

"How so?" she asks gently. It is the gentleness of hope, and beneath that a hunger, one the Australian can feel in himself: a hard jab in his guts. But what she wants is not his to give. He will never be enough. "What did you mess up?" she asks again. "Please tell me."

Whatever anguish the Australian experienced by being apart from his son, it was Fiona who carried the greatest burden of his disappearance. She must have had to explain to Maximus why his father was suddenly gone, and that while he would come back to New York, he would never come back to them. Pigeons are perched atop a skylight at the top of the stairwell. He focuses on their coos and chortles in an attempt to ground himself in place and time, but a large piece of himself, the part to which he is attempting to affix the sound, is missing.

"Tell me," says Fiona, again. "What did you mess up?"

"Life," says the Australian. "Look," he adds, before Fiona can argue or try to console him. "I want to see Maximus today."

After planning a visit for 1 p.m., Fiona asks where he is staying.

"With friends," he says.

Fiona invites him to come stay at the pop star's house. "Just for a while," she says. "Until you have, you know, something."

"No need."

There is a silence during which Fiona might be crying. In the past, her crying has mystified the Australian, but this time he understands. She had fallen in love with him and, for years, cultivated that love despite his inability to truly reciprocate. She believed in the promise that she and the Australian would always have each other, only to eventually realize she never had him to begin with.

"OK," she says. "Let me know if you change your mind."

"Thanks. Will do."

"Goodbye."

"Bye."

Thick clots of snow are landing on the skylight. The pigeons have flown away. The stairwell is freezing. The Australian wishes he were in Geelong, the seaside town of his childhood, lying on the fine white sand of a beach there. He sits on a cement step, holding his knees and shivering, and lets his desire expand—all across Australia, out over the South Pacific and Indian oceans, and around the entire Southern Hemisphere until it contains every inch of the planet where, today, it is warm.

The Australian tries to open the loft door and finds that he has locked himself out. It is 7:21 a.m.. He sits shivering until eight o'clock, at which time he can reasonably assume that somebody inside will be awake. When he knocks, it is Emmanuel who answers. "Oh," he says, with obvious disdain. "We were wondering where you went."

In the open space of the kitchen, Willam is slicing strawberries into a mixing bowl while Celeste feeds carrots into an industrial-sized stainless-steel juicer.

"Welcome back," she says cheerfully. "I hope you're hungry."

"I appreciate it, really. I don't want to impose," says the Australian.

"Nonsense," says William, sprinkling sugar over the sliced strawberries. Beside the bowl, steam rises from a pile of powdered sugar–dusted crêpes. "We demand that you join us. Mandatory Saturday treat!"

Emmanuel has been glaring at the Australian since his reentry. Five placemats are on the kitchen table. "Breakfast sounds lovely." The Australian is, in fact, starving. "Thank you."

While Celeste arranges plates, William punches a text message into his phone. Atlas appears from his bedroom. He reaches the dining area, and everyone sits. Atlas puts on his empty plate what looks like a candy bar in a black wrapper.

"What've you got there?" asks the Australian.

Without looking up from his lap, Atlas slowly turns the bar to reveal its label: SPACE FOOD STICKS: PEANUT BUTTER—and then below, in smaller print, DEVELOPED FOR THE U.S. SPACE PROGRAM.

Celeste smiles and says, "Bon appétit!"

The crêpes are thin and buttery, the strawberries ripe and sweet. The carrot juice is perfect, too, and drinking it sparks an idea in the Australian that perhaps he will work in a health food shop. He will prepare fresh-squeezed juices, smoothies, and shots of wheatgrass alongside lean, smiling younger people with abundant body hair. Everyone will be friends and will have sex with each other. Of course, this new lifestyle will not solve all of the Australian's problems, but eventually, after a few weeks, at least he will perk up enough to have feral sex with one of his coworkers—a twenty-four-year-old woman whose hippie parents named her something like Paisley or Karma or Crystal. The Australian will say to her, "I'm just not in a place right now where I can be seriously involved," and she will laugh and put up her hand, dirty with actual dirt from tending a rooftop herb garden, and say, "Whoa, man. Chill. I don't believe in monogamy. It's like, you can't own another soul, you know?"

The fantasy shatters when the Australian's fork clinks against his empty plate. He is still famished. Celeste and William have eaten less than half of their meals, and Atlas has taken only a few nibbles of his Space Food Stick.

Emmanuel, who hasn't touched his food, is staring at the Australian with eyes narrowed into hateful slits. "You eat like an animal with rabies," he says.

Celeste and William feebly scold their son, which sends Emmanuel into another fury. As the Australian watches the back and forth, rage accumulates within him—at Emmanuel for his malice, at Celeste and William for their lack of control, and at himself for being at the mercy of these people, and ultimately the whims of the world. His anger and hunger band together, becoming one overwhelming urge to howl. He bangs his fist on the tabletop. It is louder than he expected, and the family starts.

"Emmanuel is right," says the Australian. "A very astute lad, indeed." Plate in hand, he stands and walks over to the kitchen counter. "I eat like an animal because I *am* an animal." He serves himself a large pile of strawberries and layers crêpes over them—four, five, six—without bothering to fold them or dust them with powdered sugar.

The entire family is frozen.

"We're all animals," the Australian says, placing his huge second breakfast on the table. "Didn't they teach you that in school?" He forks an entire crêpe into his mouth. "Want to know what really gets me foaming at the mouth?" he asks, muffled by food.

Emmanuel's eyes dart toward each of his parents, whose eyes are fixed on the Australian.

"Want to know what's really killing me? Nobody needs me." He spears another crêpe. "Not one person in the world." He shoves the entire thing in his mouth. After a few cursory chews, he swallows it. "You want to put me down? Put me out of my misery?" He looks straight at Emmanuel, who immediately lowers his gaze. "Give it your best shot. Slay me." He puts down his fork. "I'm easy. Go ahead."

Emmanuel rises slowly from his seat, head bowed. "Excuse me," he whispers. "I'm sorry." He walks to his bedroom in small, quick steps and shuts the door behind him.

Atlas looks up from his lap, eyes wide and bright, and he laughs—one loud, triumphant *ha*.

The Australian stands in the foyer of the pop star's East Sixty-Third Street brownstone, which is actually two large brownstones that have been combined into a mansion. He was let in by one of the pop star's assistants, a cherubic young woman wearing tan jodhpurs and a white silk blouse, who has vanished up a spiral staircase in search of Fiona. The pop star is nowhere in sight. The Australian imagines her sequestered upstairs in a master bedroom, heavy curtains drawn, lying in bed with cucumber slices covering her eyes. Maybe incense burns at some kind of shrine.

Maximus squeals from somewhere above. "Daddy?" he cries out.

"That's right," says Fiona, whose feet appear at the top of the floral-carpeted staircase. "We're going to see Daddy. Don't run. Here—hold my hand, sweetheart."

They begin to descend. When Maximus is fully visible, the Australian steps out of the foyer into the marble-floored reception area at the base of the staircase. He outstretches his arms. "Where's my boy?"

A big, open-mouthed smile spreads across Maximus's face.

"No running on the stairs," says Fiona, letting go of his hand.

"Daddy!" Maximus pads down the last few steps. "Here I am, Daddy!"

"Can't wait to take you out for some fun!" The Australian picks up his son, swings him in the air, hugs him to his chest. Maximus's fingers clutch the back of the Australian's neck tightly and his small, sturdy legs wrap around the Australian's waist. He closes his eyes and smells the familiar, soapy scent of his son's hair. "My boy," he says, blinking against tears. If only this moment could be an entry point into a new life, one consisting only of touch and warmth.

Maximus presses his hands against the Australian's chest, then wriggles and shimmies down to the ground. The Australian crouches and reaches out his hand but Maximus darts out of the room, into a parlor to the right of the foyer, a dimly lit room strewn with toys: a miniature fire engine and tiny police cars, wooden building blocks, and various superhero figurines.

"There he goes," says Fiona, smiling. "I'm sorry. You know—that's just what kids do."

The Australian nods and follows her through the arched entryway into the parlor, where they stand watching Maximus. Sitting on his knees, he flies a Batman figurine over a coffee table and a stack of art gallery catalogues on the floor beside it. One large and two mid-sized Victorian paintings hang on the walls, all depicting fairies—perfectly proportioned winged women whose tiny stature can only be apprehended in relation to other, peripheral figures: a rotund bluebird, a comparatively gigantic man playing a lute, a towering mushroom.

"Sweetie," Fiona calls out to Maximus, who continues to zoom his Batman figurine through the air. "Did you know that your daddy used to be Superman—an Australian version of Superman?" She leans against the entryway, resting her head against it.

"No he didn't," says Maximus, laughing. "That can't happen!" He drops the figurine and begins pushing the fire engine across the carpet.

"Why can't it happen?" asks the Australian. Sensing that Fiona is looking at him, he forces his face to relax.

"Superman can fly," says Maximus. "He can do anything." He stops his play and eyes his father. "You can only do some things." He shrugs. "You're just a regular man."

"Can we talk alone for a bit?" Fiona asks the Australian. "Stella can watch Maximus. We'll come back in a few minutes."

"Sure," he says.

The Australian and Fiona leave Maximus under the watch of the pop star's assistant. Fiona leads the way through the house, past the staircase and a second parlor gilded with platinum records, golden trophies, and, on a glass table, purple and blue hydrangeas gathered in a crystal vase. They pass through a formal dining room lined with tropical fish tanks into a kitchen at the back of the house.

Fiona opens the refrigerator and removes an unlabeled glass bottle filled with murky brown liquid. "Kombucha," she says, adding that the pop star rarely drinks anything else. "It's fermented tea with some other stuff. It's got healthy mold on the bottom."

The Australian raises an eyebrow.

"It's good," she says, shrugging. "Hippie stuff. Don't make fun of me."

She opens the bottle and takes a sip, then offers it to him. To his surprise, he likes it—its tartness and fizziness and slightly boozy aftertaste—and Fiona hands him his own bottle. They sit across from each other halfway down the kitchen table.

"So these friends you're staying with," says Fiona. "Do I know them?"

"I don't really know them, honestly. Just a lady I met on my trip." The idea of explaining that the lady is Celeste exhausts him. "I crashed with her and her family. It was a one-night thing."

The Australian fled Celeste's loft directly after his outburst at breakfast, neglecting to bring his duffel bag with him. He must go fetch it, but then where will he go?

"Finn and Vivian are out of town," he says. "But I may be able to stay at their place in Park Slope, with Michelle and Laurent. Do you know about that whole deal?"

Fiona nods.

"I need to call again," says the Australian. Fiona looks worried. "If that falls through, I'll sort it out."

Fiona cups her hands around her bottle of kombucha. "You know you can always stay here," she says.

The Australian is silent.

"Why won't you?"

"I can't," he replies softly.

Fiona's concern turns to visible agitation. "But why?" She holds up a hand. "Just listen," she says. "I jumped the gun, asking for a divorce. I had so much going on. It felt like everything was falling down on me. And what happened with your mother—it just came out of nowhere. I was too rigid. I treated you like I treated my family when I moved to New York—like I needed to make a clean break, a dramatic exit. God, I wish I could take it back. Maximus and I should have come to Melbourne with you. We are a family. I want to see if we can mend things—for us, and for Maximus. Please stay here."

The Australian lowers his head to his hands. "Fiona, you deserve better. We both know that."

"Oh please," she says. "That is a total cop-out."

"You were right to kick me out," he says. "It's the best thing you could have done, for me too. I've got to get my act together."

Fiona's looks crestfallen. "I've spoken with a lawyer," she says, her voice trembling. "If we're not going to fight each other, we can work out everything through her. Are we going to fight?"

The Australian looks her in the eyes. Perhaps mentioning a lawyer is a test meant to expose his stance as a bluff. "No fighting," he says. "I want to spend a decent amount of time with Maximus. So long as there's no debate over that, no fighting."

Fiona assures him that she understands his importance to Maximus and would never undercut that. "I know how much you suffer," she says. "You never talk about it, but I know what not having a father has done to you. I could always feel this—this terrible pain." She wipes the condensation from her bottle with her sleeve. "Anger, too."

She continues speaking about what the Australian has lost, and how much he gives Maximus despite it all. Fiona reaches the end of her speech, and the Australian mutters, "Thank you."

"Is that the only jacket you have with you?" She frowns at his wind-breaker. "I put just about everything in storage. I'm sorry—I couldn't drag it all here. Whenever you want, I'll give you the key to the unit and you can go retrieve your things. But you're going to take Maximus now, yes?" She gets up from her chair and strides out of the kitchen. A moment later, she returns holding a puffy black parka with a logo embroidered on the breast: a tiny red rose. "You'll need something warmer."

The Australian spends the next several hours whirling around the city with Maximus. First, they go to an ice skating rink set up outside of a chic hotel in Chelsea only during the winter months, a miniature oval of ice meant just for children, where Maximus falls on his bottom intentionally, repeatedly, shrieking with delight each time. They get hot cocoas at a French chocolate confections shop, Li-Ly, where Maximus slurps twice from his thick, creamy beverage and is done. On the walk to their next destination, the Australian phones Michelle and Laurent, who welcome him to spend the night, adding that they will be out until 7:30 p.m. and that he can arrive anytime thereafter. At a bookstore, the Australian reads aloud from an oversized book about an unlikely friendship between a seahorse and a starfish, and a few rhyming poems from a children's anthology, both of which the Australian ultimately purchases. Then Maximus becomes absorbed in playing with stuffed animals and scribbling on a pad with markers provided in the children's section.

The Australian's desire for Maximus's happiness has become panicked. In a boutique toy store called Kinderland, Maximus sees lunch boxes for the first time and is so enamored by the notion of carrying his lunch to school in a shiny tin container painted with the grinning face of a monkey or a space explorer wearing a jet pack that the Australian cannot resist buying him not one or two but three, using his debit card and thereby diminishing his bank account to double digits. They climb a rocky hill in Central Park to watch the sunset, a blue and orange haze dwindling beyond a slope of naked trees. After paying cash to vendors for chili dogs followed by funnel cakes, the Australian's wallet contains just eighteen dollars, and he now has a total of ninety-four dollars to his name.

The Australian and Maximus leave Central Park hand in hand, beginning their walk back to the pop star's house. As they pass through the park's exit onto Central Park East, the Australian feels a more intense gravitational pull on his lungs and stomach. It is another freezing night, and he is grateful for the parka Fiona gave him. One block east of the park, Maximus stops in his tracks and drops the Australian's hand.

"Mommy says you went to Australia because your mom was sick," he says. "Is she better now?"

The Australian has never discussed death with his son and wonders whether Fiona has. Perhaps the closest Maximus has ever come to experiencing death in any immediate way was his father's two-week disappearance to Melbourne. This is an important moment, one that requires grace, but the Australian can't straighten out his mind enough to craft a delicate answer.

"My mother was very sick," he says. The words that come next simply appear, puffs of white breath hanging in the air. "A very sad thing happened during my trip. She died."

Maximus is silent for a moment. He fingers the collar of his navy wool pea coat. "What happens when someone dies?" he asks.

"When a person is old and they get very sick," says the Australian, "sometimes they don't get better."

Maximus's eyes widen, and the Australian realizes he has misspoken. He absolutely cannot speak of his own conception of death: that the soul evaporates up and away when the brainwaves flatline, and either flame or time takes care of the rest.

"When an old person is done living on Earth," he says, "they go to sleep and dream about Heaven. Heaven is a place full of love and beautiful flowering fields, and all of the person's favorite things, and the dream lasts forever. When someone dies, we don't get to see them anymore, and that's sad, but the person who has died is in the most wonderful place in the universe, so that's happy."

Maximus appears thoughtful for a long moment, and then shrugs. They continue walking.

As they wind crosstown and a few blocks south, the Australian wishes he could have handled the conversation better. Should he have told Maximus to talk to Fiona? Or would she have approved of his approach? He doesn't know. He senses the presence of the photograph in its leather sleeve, tucked inside his knapsack. If Lock Jones had ever answered this question for the Australian, would he have done a better job of it? It seems unlikely that any parent knows precisely how to explain mortality to a three-year-old.

As he helps Maximus climb the ice-slicked steps of the pop star's brownstone, the cherubic assistant opens the front door. She is hanging their jackets in a closet when the pop star appears at the entrance of the foyer, some six feet from the Australian.

"Hello!" she shouts. She is barefoot, wearing a chocolate-colored velour sweatsuit. "It's been ages!"

At first the shouting is disconcerting, but then the Australian remembers her micropsia, and realizes that he must appear to her very distant, a miniscule man at the entrance of her endlessly expansive dwelling. The assistant rushes to a fireplace near the bottom of the stairs and plucks a pair of copper, wire-framed spectacles from the mantel. She places them on the pop star's face, carefully tucking the frames' temples behind the pop star's ears. The right rim has no lens, while the lens of the left eye is thick—its surface refracted, cutting light from the chandelier overhead into bright, spectral colors.

"Ah, that's better," says the pop star at a slightly lower volume, still louder than necessary. "The doctors have me wearing this prism thingy now." She points to the spectacles. "How strange! Well, it's good to see you." She reaches for the Australian's hand and overshoots, grazing his abdomen.

"You, too," he says, stepping back and taking her hand.

The assistant explains that Fiona is out running errands, and it is unknown when she will return.

"I'll wait for her, if that's all right," says the Australian. He needs to buy time before continuing on to the Park Slope apartment. He has two hours until he is expected.

"Sure, that's fine," says the assistant. "Make yourself at home."

She takes Maximus upstairs for a bath, and the Australian walks back to the second parlor, adorned with the pop star's career memorabilia and the vases and pots of flowers. The pop star follows him. He sits down on the sofa and she lowers herself very slowly into a leather armchair facing him. She leans back, deep into the leather, and crosses one leg over the other. "So, what kind of trouble have you been getting yourself into?"

Tired from the afternoon's excursion, the Australian offers a meek shrug.

"Fiona is very upset," she snaps. "She is, in fact, distraught. Dismayed. Heartbroken. She is hiding from you now, but you must know that."

The Australian shakes his head.

"What did you expect? You are leaving her alone with the child."

"She's not alone," says the Australian gruffly. It requires deliberate effort on his part not to raise his voice to match the pop star's decibels. "I'm back in New York now. I'll spend time with Maximus, have him at my place when I have one, however much she'll let me."

The pop star shakes her head slowly, exuding both pity and contempt. "Fiona is my girl," she says. "If you have any question about whose side I'm on, I'll answer right now—I'm on her side."

"There are no sides. Everything is amicable."

"Oh, please." The pop star waves a hand. "That's what everyone says these days. There are no sides. We're still friends. Mindful uncoupling. It makes me want to wretch." She pulls her spectacles from her face and holds them at arm's length. "These things," she says, shouting again now. She squints at the Australian. "The doctors tell me to wear them, but I can't stand it. When I first put them on they help a bit, but after a while they make me horrendously dizzy." She places them on the table beside a vase of hydrangea. "I hear you won't be staying with us. Tell me, where are you deigning to reside?"

The Australian takes a deep breath, trying to hold onto his composure, but a deep trembling seizes hold of his core. The pop star's remarks about him abandoning Fiona and Maximus are unfair. "I'm staying with Celeste," he says vindictively. He stops there, waiting for the pop star to soak in his words.

"Celeste who?" she asks. "Is she a new girlfriend?"

"Just *Celeste*—no last name," he replies. "You know her, I'm sure."

The pop star looks stunned, but quickly regains her composure. "Of course," she says, smiling curtly.

The Australian recounts how he met Celeste at the country club in Yamba and the instant connection they shared. As he speaks, the pop star looks theatrically indifferent, but the Australian notices her twisting a big moonstone ring around her right pinky, over and over. "It was just one of those things," he says. "One of those rare introductions where you feel like you've known someone forever. She's a good, giving person. And very wise. Soulful—that's the word, I'd say."

The pop star looks stricken, pale.

"I stayed with her and her family last night," he adds. "We had strawberry crêpes for breakfast, and the most delicious fresh-squeezed carrot juice. It was lovely. But I don't want to impose, so tonight I'll stay elsewhere."

The pop star tucks her legs up onto her chair and hugs her knees, contracting into a ball. The Australian is alarmed by how fragile she appears, how little. Her lips are pursed, her eyes shut. He fears she is about to cry. It seems possible that she would dare say something spiteful about him to Maximus. That she would poison his sweet, young mind with the notion that his father is abandoning him—or that he betrayed Fiona. The pop star's shoulders shake, and a tear runs down her cheek.

"I'm sorry," says the Australian. He excuses himself from the parlor, retrieves his parka from the closet in the foyer, and lets himself out of the house.

———

The elevator to Celeste's apartment opens directly into the loft's dining area, and she is standing beside the table waiting for the Australian when he arrives.

"Pardon me," he says. "I just have to collect my belongings, and then I'll get going."

Celeste walks up to him. "I don't want you to worry about what happened today." She places her hands on his shoulders and squeezes. "In fact, I owe you a major thank you."

She explains that, after the Australian departed, Atlas began to speak—chatting away about comic books, a girl in his class he has a crush on, and a science project he would like to do for an upcoming interscholastic fair. Emmanuel stayed locked in his room for over two hours, and when he emerged he was pleasant to his family for the first time in months. Now William has taken both boys out for egg creams.

"You had a magical effect on them," says Celeste. "You were honest. Totally blunt. Atlas seemed to have woken up. He's finally back in our lives. I mean, once he started talking we couldn't get him to stop. And Emmanuel! He must have needed someone to shrink him down to size. He's himself again. No more of that belligerent arrogance act." She releases the Australian's shoulders and takes a step back. "I'm imploring you not to leave. Stay here, please—unless, of course, you have other plans."

The Australian feels, for the first time in a long while, useful. The idea of integrating himself into the lush ecosystem of Celeste's family unit, albeit temporarily, warms him. Also, the journey out to the apartment in Park Slope would require three subway transfers and a long, uphill walk in the freezing cold.

Sitting in the living room, the Australian explains Fiona's relationship to the pop star and describes his own encounter with her today. "I know you've been a target of her anger in the past," he says. "Do you have any idea why she hates me?"

"I do know her, quite well actually. We both came into our careers at around the same time. She's always been fragile—painfully shy. I don't think people realize that. When we were in our twenties, she was agoraphobic. She only ever left her apartment for professional obligations. She despises me because—well, I'm not really sure. She perceives me as a threat, but in what way I can't imagine. We've had different trajectories, totally divergent paths. I was a model, she a singer, so we were never in competition. But she always acted as though we were. I tried to make relations pleasant with her—to no avail, unfortunately. And honestly, I have no patience for her anymore."

"Do you think she feels threatened by me, too?" asks the Australian.

Celeste smiles. "Not quite," she says. "I think she bristles because she sees herself in you, and it makes her uncomfortable." She pauses, studying his face. "You both radiate hope," she says. "Intensely."

Across the loft, the elevator doors slide open. William, Atlas, and Emmanuel spill out, all of them laughing. Celeste smiles and waves at them, then turns back to the Australian. She leans in toward him.

"Hope is a wonderful thing to have," she says. "It'll hurt you, but the world really needs it."

While the Australian feels like an intruder, he can concede that he serves a function in the home. This is especially true on the Australian's third evening in the loft, when Celeste and William are out to dinner. The Australian, Emmanuel, and Atlas sit on the living room couch eating microwaved edamame and watching *The Mutator*, a film about a young man, Duo, who lives 150 years in the future. Duo is able to see into the future and to alter people's DNA with his mind. He strives to use his powers only for good, to change the fate of those otherwise genetically destined to suffer illness, for example, or to render infertile those whose offspring would be fated to become serial killers. Meanwhile, a secret agency is determined to obtain a sample of Duo's DNA—a drop of blood, spit, sweat, or semen; a skin cell, fingernail clipping, or hair—without Duo knowing he is being targeted. The agency's plan is to clone him and then harness the clone's capabilities to disable the leaders of every nation on Earth, seize governance of the entire planet, enslave all but the wealthiest people and sell the slaves to corporations.

Midway through the film, the Australian zones out. Maximus must be tucked into bed by now, all those many long blocks uptown. Earlier, the Australian took him to a park. They built a snowman, then read books at the pop star's house. The two-hour visit was not enough, but the Australian feels pressure to spend time with Emmanuel and Atlas in order to earn his keep. He looks away from the flatscreen plasma television and out a window at the snow, which is falling in flurries. How many pigeons are there in New York City? What shelter is there for all of those tens or hundreds of thousands—or millions? It seems remarkable to the Australian how infrequently one comes across a dead pigeon, given their proliferation and the disaffection the city shows them. He turns back to *The Mutator*. Duo has finally realized that the government agency wants his DNA and is explaining to his love interest, Priya, that there is no way he can mutate all of the agents' genetic code in time to disable or kill them, which is the only way to save the planet and himself.

"Why doesn't he just kill himself? *That* would save the world," says Emmanuel. "Like, throw himself into a volcano. No one could steal his DNA out of molten lava."

"I think he should steal a space shuttle," Atlas chimes in. "He can just live the rest of his life in outer space." He pauses for a moment before adding, "And he could bring some friends. Or marry Priya and bring her. They could live in the space shuttle, or make a settlement on a planet in a distant galaxy. Whatever they want."

The Australian turns to face the boys. "Duo has to stay because he's a hero. There's more to being a hero than the absence of harm. He has to take action."

"Why?" asks Atlas.

"Well, that's just how movies work. And real life, too. We may live in the United States, France, Uganda, Sri Lanka, wherever—but we are citizens of the world," he says, roused by the inspiration and hypocrisy of his own words. "It's not enough to leave the world the same. Our job is to make it better."

PART SIX

FINN CALLS THE AUSTRALIAN to say he is back in town. That evening they meet for drinks at the Proletariat, a bar whose walls are plastered with replicated Soviet propaganda posters and whose floor is covered with sawdust. Only vodka is offered, and though there are twelve different brands, every shot is the same ridiculous price. The Australian and Finn perch side by side on stools at the graffiti-carved bar, where they are served by a bartender who—owing to his scarf, full lips, and lustrous, tousled hair—bears a striking resemblance to the photograph of the young Karl Marx above the cash register.

The Australian tells Finn everything that has happened since they last saw each other, ending with his current living situation. "Celeste is feeding me and letting me stay with her, wash my clothes in her laundry room, sleep in her office. She loaned me a thousand bucks," he says, closing his eyes and massaging the bridge of his nose. "She insisted I take it. It's very kind of her, obviously, but it's crushing me. I'm a charity case."

Finn pats the Australian's back and orders them another round. When their shots arrive, both men knock them back, slam their shot glasses on the bar, and then sit silently until the burn of alcohol in their throats subsides.

"I'm going to ask you something," says Finn. "This is not a charitable offering. This is not a bailout. I genuinely want your help. Before I tell you what I'm talking about, you have to swear this will stay between us just for now."

The Australian nods, leaning in toward his friend. "Of course," he says. "Who would I tell?"

Finn explains that funding for his new salon was harder to come by than he had anticipated. Just when he thought his dream was squashed, a major investor emerged.

"Who?" asks the Australian.

"A producer," Finn says. "A Hollywood producer. She's behind a reality show called *Snipped*. Have you seen it?"

The Australian shakes his head.

"Each season is shot in a different salon," says Finn, "but the gist is that a salon owner has a bunch of stylists working under him or her, and at the end of each episode one of them gets fired and replaced by a new hire. And of course there's drama that goes on between the stylists, the fucking and fighting and all that. The show's been airing for three seasons now, and every salon they've featured is still in business, so that's a good omen, I think. The television network wants to help me open my salon. This producer, she really believes in me, man. They're going to invest in my business, and they'll get to shoot the show there for a season. That's the deal."

"Wow," says the Australian. "This is a great thing, right?"

"Yeah, I think it could be an amazing opportunity for exposure—for my salon, and for us. Me and you."

"I'm thrilled, Finn. I don't know anything about reality TV pro-grams, but you deserve all the exposure in the world. Wonderful news, mate," he says, shaking his friend's hand vigorously. "But what does this have to do with me?"

The Australian takes a job at Finn's salon in Williamsburg, his first full-time employment since working on Wall Street. The salon is called Glossary. Clients must define themselves in three words, and stylists give them hairdos inspired by those definitions. Starting from the grand opening in mid-February, camera and production crews are a constant presence. By the middle of the first week, the Austra-lian is convinced that his new position, salon coordinator, is a sham. The miscellaneous tasks Finn assigns him—ordering smocks, picking a font for the signage, arranging flowers at the front desk, dropping the rent check in the mail—strike him as foolish. Finn insists these duties are crucial, however, and the Australian plays along.

Initially, doing his so-called work in front of the cameras is em-barrassing, and during the long lulls between his duties he hides in the stockroom, but a week into filming, he has become more or less numb to the surveillance. Although the first episode of *Snipped* won't air for another few weeks, it is clear that its focus will be the ris-ing tensions between the stylists. Tammy, a thirty-something former model from LA with a whiny voice and a nose job, brings her Maltese to work. Úrsula, a Portuguese woman in her forties, has a penchant for harsh, geometric hairstyles and tirelessly criticizes America. To-bias, an emotionally hypersensitive ex-farmhand from Kansas, has no formal training in hair styling. Sharon, who goes by the nickname Mama Bama, is a white conservative Republican from Tuscaloosa with a bodybuilder husband and fraternal triplet sons. And finally

Ronald, an elderly African American man with braces on his teeth, wears a wool poncho every day and smudges not only his own workstation but those to his left and right as well with sage incense each morning. The stylists go to outrageous lengths to sabotage each other and to impress upon Finn their own talents and savvy. In special scenes called Professional Confessionals, he confides to the camera the shortcomings and virtues of each.

The rivalries between the stylists strike the Australian as a sort of warped Darwinism, a process of unnatural selection: survival of the weirdest. At the end of week one, with all of the stylists standing in a row before him, Finn fires Sharon, a.k.a. Mama Bama, for singeing a client's hair with bleach—"I'm sorry, but you've been snipped," he says, as per the show's guidelines—and on the following Monday she is replaced by Evan, a self-proclaimed sex god and tarot card devotee who wears violet contact lenses and talks endlessly about his hairless cat.

The Australian visits Maximus at the pop star's house most evenings, continues to reside at Celeste and William's loft, and has developed a buoyant friendship with Emmanuel and Atlas. The three of them give each other noogies, watch action movies, tell dirty jokes. Sometimes the Australian believes he is indeed a salutary influence, while other times he worries that his enjoyment of the diversions he shares with the boys is due to his own gradual degeneration into a teenager. Or, worse, that no degeneration was needed at all. When Celeste and William happen to witness the Australian joshing around with their sons, his ears burn red. His unease is kept at bay by the fact that he is using nearly all of his wages, which are generous thanks to Finn and *Snipped*'s producers, to pay off his credit card debts. It is an adult, responsible thing to do—and, gradually, he is doing it.

———

When the show begins to air in mid-March, the Australian is rec-ognized on the subway a few times, and a couple more times on the street. Otherwise, his life is unaffected by the public nature of his employment, and he is glad. He watches the premiere episode of *Snipped* with Celeste, William, Emmanuel, and Atlas. Although his appearances are restricted to cameos, seeing himself on national television is alarming and he swears never to watch it again. The sa-lon coordinator job is a strange limbo—certainly he won't work at Glossary forever—and he daydreams between chores about what his future might hold. The only way he can envision any life for himself in New York City is to picture a small moment shared with Maximus. Imagined scenes with the two of them—riding the sub-way, browsing the shelves of a public library, roller skating, viewing fossilized dinosaur bones at the Museum of Natural History—are the only ones that make sense.

However, no one will pay him for loving his son. He will need a real career, an apartment. The more he dwells on these obligations, the more compelled he is to retreat into fantasy. He takes to bringing to work one or two of the *Australian Geographic Outdoor* magazines and perusing them during free moments. As he flips through their pages, he transposes himself over the strong, sun-bronzed men depict-ed therein—backpacking in the Tingle forests in Australia's southwest, big-wave kayaking off the Queensland coast, running marathons in the Outback, spearfishing off the Solitary Islands dotting Coffs Har-bour in New South Wales. Men out in the wilderness, using their lungs to maximum potential, with no thoughts in their minds except: *Go*.

One morning, Fiona calls the Australian and asks him to skip work and take Maximus for the day. "I was up all night with a stom-ach flu," she says. "My boss is flying out to a spa in Zurich today for this stupid color-enhanced flotation treatment and she's bringing all of the assistants with her. I can't find a babysitter. I've got a fever and I can't keep anything down. I need the rest."

The Australian explains that he is contractually obligated to be at Glossary, but he could bring Maximus. He would have to sign a waiver and permissions allowing Maximus to be filmed, but would do his best to keep him off camera.

"Jesus," says Fiona. "All right."

Maximus tags along with him on a few errands, watches some haircuts and dye jobs, banters with several of the stylists, pokes around the stockroom, and then naps on a cushioned bench in the break room. The Australian coaxes him to sleep using a hairclip as a impromptu puppet, opening and closing the metal tongs in sync with each word of an improvised song about sleep being fun, which he rhymes with "warm yellow sun." The producers would not acquiesce to the Australian's request that he and Maximus not be filmed, but then again, he didn't press very hard because it didn't seem worth fussing over, and he pays the crew little notice. His repartee with his toddler son is hardly the sensational content people tune in for. When he drops Maximus off with Fiona that evening, he has nothing significant to report.

At the same New Zealand farm where the Australian saw a ewe give birth over twenty years ago, there were also chickens enclosed in a wire pen. Standing atop a small hill, perhaps twenty paces away, he observed them clucking and pecking lazily. He moved closer to get a better look at them. The chickens suddenly congregated into a flock and rushed toward him. Inside the pen, right in front of the Australian's feet, they crammed against each other, squawking loudly. It was amusing, but also gave him a special feeling—a sense of absolute dominion, which was novel to him and which he has never felt again. He stepped over the wire enclosure and stood amongst them. He had been studying Greek mythology in school, and as he dropped pieces of corn into the bobbling swarm, he felt just like Zeus tossing lightning bolts from atop Mount Olympus.

That moment comes to the Australian's mind as the antithesis of his shocking experience, on a clammy gray morning late in March, when he is swarmed by fans. He arrives at Glossary to find the usual crowd outside, perhaps fifteen women and four or five men—but instead of ignoring him like usual, they encircle him. One woman, petite and wearing a faux fur coat, shoves a permanent marker in the Australian's face and yanks up her shirt, indicating that she wants him to autograph the flesh of her belly. Another woman, middle-aged and garishly made up, shouts, "Please! Please!" but the Australian has no idea what she wants. "Hey, Daddy," purrs a man with a goatee, caressing the sleeve of the Australian's parka.

The Australian dashes into the salon, where he discovers that Finn and the stylists have been watching through the front window. "What the hell is going on?" he asks.

"Didn't you watch last night? You're a star!" says Finn.

Before the Australian can speak, the stylists begin applauding him, except for Úrsula, who, as always, looks disgusted by everyone and everything. The Australian pinches Finn's shirtsleeve and leads him to the relative privacy of the break room, where he learns that the previous night's episode heavily featured the day that Maximus visited Glossary.

"That song," says Finn, wide-eyed. "The one you sang to Maximus with the hair clip—it was brilliant. They love you, man."

"Who loves me?" asks the Australian.

"Everyone." Finn slaps the Australian's chest. "The stylists, people on the Internet, those people outside. America!"

"You've gone mental," says the Australian.

Finn shakes his head, still grinning. "You really have no idea."

It is only when the Australian returns to the loft after work that he begins to appreciate the magnitude of what has transpired. The moment he steps out of the elevator, Atlas shouts: "He's here!"

"Come! Sit, sit, sit," shouts Emmanuel, waving him over to the living room. "Bro, you broke the Internet! You're totally dominating social media. You're all over the place. You're a meme!"

"A what?" asks the Australian.

"A meme," Atlas chimes in. "You don't know what a meme is?"

The Australian admits that he does not.

"Well," says Atlas, "there's this picture of you singing with the hairclip, and people made up captions for it."

"What do they say?" asks the Australian.

"All kinds of stuff," says Emmanuel. "Like, I saw one that said, 'Praying he's sing-le!' And this other one said, 'Aussie gets hot, singing to a tot.'"

The boys double over with laughter.

"Are the people writing these things batshit?" asks the Australian.

"Yeah, but that doesn't matter," says Atlas. "Dude, you're on TV, too. Like, the news. And check out what we found. Hold on a sec!" He runs to his bedroom and returns with a laptop. He opens it on the coffee table and types quickly on the keyboard. "Okay," he says, turning the screen to face the Australian.

The browser is open to a hastily assembled webpage: HottieAussieDaddy.com. The garish main page features the Australian and Maximus in silhouette and links to fans' imagined romantic encounters with the Australian.

"It's called fan fiction," says Emmanuel. "See, people can send in stories about you where they pretend you're their boyfriend. And other people's boyfriend, too—like the stylists. And even Finn."

"Check this out," Atlas says, typing away again. On the gossip website *Ogler* he clicks on an article dated today entitled "Top 10 Sexiest Dads on TV."

The Australian's face appears on the laptop screen. In this picture, his eyes gaze down tenderly—a still shot of a moment in which he was looking at his sleeping son—and beneath that image, the headline: "DILF=Dad I'd Like to $%&*." The Australian feels foggy and sick.

"You're famous, dude!" Emmanuel says.

"So epic," says Atlas, elbowing the Australian in the ribs.

Emmanuel nods in agreement. "Totally epic."

The Australian finds himself tumbling through treacherous terrain, his days carved into jagged peaks and breakneck slopes by gusts of anxiety brought on by having acquired a public persona overnight. At any point in the past, had he been asked whether he would enjoy the attention of strangers, he would have said yes. In years past, he has yearned to acquire some degree of celebrity, but now that it has happened, it is incommodious and degrading. The problem is not the fans and anti-fans that try to engage him in the streets, the remixes of his naptime song that have flooded the Internet, or the inclusion of his face on a new billboard in Times Square advertising *Snipped*. It is the fact that, in a very specific and reductive way, he has become a known entity.

The Australian's being is no longer confined to his own consciousness and those of the handful of people who know him in the first degree—who have either warmed to him or resented and disliked him. Either way, it was due to the realities of his character. Now his existence extends into the consciousness of strangers who have no interest whatsoever in his intentions or desires or his welfare, one way or another. They have glimpsed fragments of the Australian on their television screens or computers, like the glass shards of a broken taillight scattered in the street, and they believe they can ascertain the entire man to whom this sparkly refuse once belonged. It does not matter to the Australian whether people's conceptions of him are positive or negative. Either way, he abhors their inaccuracy.

Snipped's producers are ecstatic. They order the camera crew to film the Australian every moment he is at Glossary, save for his trips to the restroom. No one, including Finn, seems to understand the Australian's vexation and growing bitterness at the spotlights and hullabaloo. Everyone he knows—save for Fiona, who has forbidden Maximus ever to accompany the Australian to work again, and Celeste and William, who were wary of the reality television idea to begin with—has congratulated him repeatedly. Friends and strangers alike praise his charisma, his friendliness, his white teeth, the exceptional luster of his golden hair. It bewilders him that people seem to think that being known is, in and of itself, an achievement. He hides his face under the brim of a black baseball cap, chooses to ride in taxis instead of taking the subway, and wears sunglasses at night en route to see his son.

There seems to be no appropriate descriptor for his current status in society. He cannot be a celebrity because he has done nothing to earn the public's celebration. Nor has he done anything sufficiently terrible to warrant notoriety—and anyway, in his present condition, whether people love or hate him is a superfluous detail. The word "star" occurs to him as perhaps a cheaper designation than "celebrity," and one that could be pinned to an unworthy individual such as himself—but because he is not stalked by paparazzi and does not deliberately cultivate a fanbase, the label doesn't quite fit. Is he even a public figure? He thinks not. He doesn't live publicly, he lives privately—it is just that he happens to get filmed while doing so. The Australian accepts that there is no word, though perhaps time will invent one, for his social predicament—one akin to having some unseemly, attention-grabbing thing tacked onto his presence, like an unusually located facial piercing or a curious odor.

Because of the leap in ratings after the episode featuring the Australian and Maximus aired, Glossary is booked solid for the next six months. This ensures its survival after the end of filming in early summer. However useless the Australian feels at the salon, and however burdensome his role has become, he cannot quit. He needs his wages. Furthermore, in early April Finn signs over a small but significant percentage of ownership to the Australian—a gesture of friendship and goodwill that the Australian can't turn down.

With sufficient funds in hand, the time comes for the Australian to move out of Celeste's loft. On the night before his departure, Celeste and her family hold a festive dinner in his honor. There is champagne—sparkling apple cider for the boys—soba noodles, soy and maple-glazed pork belly, and a delicate pear tart. William toasts the Australian—"a most welcome stranger, who came into our lives and hearts and brought us all closer together. Here's to the future!"

The next morning, the Australian packs up his things, retrieves some of his possessions that Fiona put in storage, and moves into an apartment he found in the online classifieds. There, he will live with two female roommates, recent Columbia grads: Tara and Yvette. Tara is an SAT tutor for prep school kids, while Yvette works as a temp, currently employed by a hedge fund. The two women look very similar, both with long brown hair and petite figures, and the Australian has difficulty distinguishing them. The apartment is in an old townhouse in Carroll Gardens, Brooklyn, each floor now a separate apartment. The women are polite and amiable, and he is glad to see that the shared living spaces—the living room, kitchen, and two bathrooms—are minimally decorated and tidy. Unspoken boundaries quickly form between the Australian, Tara, and Yvette. If he encounters them in the kitchen or passes them in the hallway, he smiles and nods but does not initiate conversation.

April and the first half of May whir by, a blur of working at Glossary, visiting his son, and sleeping fitfully. The salon's business continues to boom. As a result, the Australian's sliver of ownership becomes a significant resource. He creates an investment account for Maximus and spends a little on rent and food. The rest he saves for as-yet unknown next steps. Restlessness rises up in him, percolating and sputtering. He is no longer a husband, which at least provided an identity, tethering him enough so that his mind could wander freely. Now, he has lost his capacity to daydream. He wants to be a genuine article of masculinity, a grade A specimen, vigorous and true—and although he hasn't the first idea what that entails, finding out starts to feel like an urgent necessity. Yet, when he looks at the world around him, all he sees are dead ends—except, of course, for the money he is accruing. He wants to use it for a worthy purpose, to enrich himself in some way. He wants to travel to—where? Where does one go to find an identity? Is there a flight he could board that would deposit him in a distant land where—there, right on the tarmac—some better version of himself would be standing, smiling and waving at him as he deplaned? The Australian doesn't want to be anywhere, yet he wants to be everywhere. He continues to read and reread the *Australian Geographic Outdoor* magazines.

The weather grows warmer, the days lengthen, and the Australian grows edgier still. He is waiting for something impossible to define. Due to his ongoing appearances on *Snipped*, people continue to recognize him on the streets. They walk up to him and begin conversing as though they know him. Instead of fleeing from the attention, the Australian begins engaging the strangers, whipping up conversation out of nothing, trying to wring something significant out of these people. Always, these encounters leave him hungry, dissatisfied. Ultimately, the thing he wants from them is not theirs to give.

At the end of May, the Australian attends Finn and Vivian's commitment ceremony, which will bind them as lovers and life partners to Michelle and Laurent. The proceedings take place in the couples' Park Slope apartment, which is furnished with framed posters from various museum shows, an upright piano, and family photos. The doorway between dining room and living room—in front of which the couples' vows are exchanged—is decorated with wildflowers for the occasion. Fiona and Maximus are in attendance, seated in the front row, and the Australian sits beside his son. The pop star is in the back row, wearing sunglasses and sucking on a candy cane. The ceremony is conducted by a female officiant whose dress looks to be made out of matted organic material, something like peat moss or lichen. Finn and Vivian stand holding hands, facing Michelle and Laurent, whose hands are also clasped.

"We are gathered here today to bear witness to a joining of hearts," the officiant begins. "As we all know, the human heart has four chambers. So together, in this joining of hearts, as these two couples exchange vows and become a quartet—a quartet of everlasting love—each four-chambered heart will join the others, and all in all we will have a sixteen-chambered heart. All of the chambers will work cooperatively, beating harmoniously—a dynamic drum circle thumping to the tune of joy and gratitude, commitment and honor."

The Australian zones out until vows are exchanged, followed by the placing of rings on each of the participants' fingers. Finn and Vivian look truly happy—Vivian having just graduated film school and found the kind of love she always wanted, Finn not only having embraced Vivian's polyamory, but having discovered a way to engage and find felicity within it, too.

The Australian is glad for them. But his own loneliness quickly undercuts that sentiment, which he feels guilty about. He glances beyond Maximus at Fiona—the bearer of every brunt of all the Australian's mistakes. She smiles at him and then returns her attention to the ceremony.

She may have pined for the Australian, but he is sure she has moved on. He studies her profile, marveling at the glow of her skin, the clarity of her brown eyes, her posture—poised and upright as always. She is doing well, he thinks. He wonders if she has a boyfriend. But why would her well-being be contingent upon a romantic relationship? All the years she lived with the Australian, she never really had him and yet she marched on. Her vitality is not due to any circumstances. No, her exuberance, that overall verdure, is rooted in the very foundation of her person, a manifestation of a truth about Fiona the Australian never appreciated before: her life is rich with meaning, found in moments big and small, and she lets resentments go—not by shoving them down, but by allowing them to slough off, revealing the light that is hers to shine.

Maximus fidgets in his seersucker suit, the legs of which are a couple inches too short. At the front of the room, all four members of the newly formed partnership lean in, a quadruple embrace. The room fills with applause. Everyone the Australian knows seems to be in the midst of their own progression. Even the pop star is now venturing outside of her home for the first time in months. All of the guests rise from their seats, still applauding. The Australian stays seated, weighed down by a new and sudden conviction: he can't wait for a destination to call to him, for a job to seek him out, for a romance to sweep him away. He must stop trying or waiting to become someone. He will start walking forward, down any path long and winding enough that he cannot see its endpoint from the outset—even one that may not have an endpoint at all.

Early in July, *Snipped* wraps up filming, but the Australian decides to stay on at Glossary until September. He feels he owes it to Finn, plus he wants to save as much money as he can. The yearning for forward motion excited within him during the commitment ceremony has stuck. He has decided to return to Australia. There, he will check up on Deedee, whom he feels he should not have left in such poor condition, and then he will follow the Dreaming Tracks—the journey his mother started but never had the chance to complete. He wants to see the parts of Australia that he has never been to: Hotham Heights in Northern Victoria, the Great Dividing Range in Gippsland,

and Nullarbor Plain—a remote and barren expanse of desert, where travelers are warned by signs stating that no water will be available for the next 770 miles. Next, he will travel to points across the globe he knows his father to have visited: Lampang, Bangkok, Hanoi, and various points in the Philippines. After that, he will continue on, surpassing the journeys of both parents, guided by a book he borrowed from Atlas during a recent dinner at Celeste and William's place: *Planet Earth's Hidden Majesty*.

When he tells Celeste, Finn, and Vivian about his intentions, they all respond with frank concern. He is emulating his father, they say, abandoning his son and shirking responsibility. To that, the Australian responds that they have it all backward. "I've always been in my father's shadow," he says. "I need to change that. I want to follow his footsteps and keep going, so that I'll finally get ahead—into the light."

His friends seem unmoved by this statement, though he is, in fact, deeply moved as he utters the words, which he practiced in his mind beforehand. He pays little mind to his friends' skepticism. What concerns him most is Fiona's reaction, and he saves the conversation with her for last. When they finally speak at the pop star's kitchen table, one month before the Australian is set to fly to Melbourne, he outlines his plan, quickly adding that he will come back to New York around Christmas—Christmas at the very least, and perhaps during the following summer as well. Fiona is distraught.

"How long will you be gone?" she asks.

"As long as it takes to work myself out," says the Australian.

"Did you actually just say that?" she asks. "I mean, seriously—do you hear yourself? Don't you see what you're doing? You are putting Maximus in the same position you were in as a kid. Jesus, how can you not see this?"

"I've got to become my best self—who I *am*—in order to be the father Maximus deserves," he says. "I need to be out in the world, which is so goddamn huge, and I need to be where I can feel that, how enormous and mysterious everything is, but I just can't here. Everything in New York is shrinking—my life, my brain. Even my body. I feel like I'm shriveling. The worst of me is everywhere I look, and there are people who recognize me wherever I go. People who praise me, if you can imagine that, for being some idiot on TV. It's killing me. I need to be in a place where I'm nobody so that I can have a fresh chance to become somebody."

All the time he is speaking, he feels as though he is watching himself from a high and distant point. His speech is the most emphatic he's ever made. When he is done, Fiona closes her eyes, wipes away tears with her fingertips.

"Please don't do this," she says. "Maximus needs you. We are his stability, his foundation—you and me."

"I'm not running away," says the Australian. "If this is ever going to be my home—the way you imagine, the way it should be—I've got to start finding my way here."

"Fuck you," whispers Fiona. "Just, fuck you."

In September, the day before the Australian is set to depart to Melbourne, he attends Maximus's fourth birthday party at a Tribeca gymnastics studio called Splitz. From the sidelines, leaning against a padded barricade, he watches Maximus and a handful of kids from his nursery school class tumble around—somersaulting, cartwheeling, bouncing off a trampoline into a pit of foam blocks, and swinging on a trapeze, elaborately harnessed and under the watch of an elven instructor named Pete. The Australian smiles faintly but does not look directly at Fiona as she walks up to the barricade and stands beside him.

"I always knew you were never really with me," she says. "And I loved you anyway. And that was my choice. It's Maximus I've been worrying about with you leaving."

The Australian lowers his head. "I don't think we're going to make much progress talking about this right now," he says.

"Just hold on," says Fiona. "I've been worried about how much Maximus will miss you—but when I stopped and thought about what you told me, your reasons for leaving, it started to make sense." She stops speaking, perhaps waiting for the Australian to respond, but he can't think of anything other than Fiona's words, which strike him has amazingly—absurdly—generous.

Across the gymnasium, Maximus runs down a matted runway, leaps onto a trampoline, and flips into the pit of foam blocks. When he scrambles out onto the mat, he looks to Fiona and the Australian, who both smile and wave.

"I'm not going to abandon Maximus," says the Australian. "I would never. You've got to know that I am not a father who would ever—"

"Come on," Fiona says. "I know you're a good dad. You don't have to tell me. I'm trying to say that, when I really think about you and your life, what's best for you and what's best for Maximus, the honest truth is I don't know what you should do. I don't know if I should be begging you to stay or throwing you a send-off party. All I know is that I understand where you're coming from." She puts her hand on the Australian's shoulder, and he turns and looks at her. "I understand that in your mind you're not really leaving. Traveling your way home—isn't that kind of what you said? And I think that is a really nice idea."

The Australian realizes Fiona is lying, an extraordinary kindness. She smiles at him, another lie. Years ago, on an early April morning, they had walked together to get pastries from Fiona's favorite bakery. As they made their way down a street lined with trees in full bloom, delicate white flowers whose centers darkened with a faint pink blush, Fiona said, "Do you know how daisies got their name?" The Australian smiled, shaking his head. "Well, the yellow center of a daisy looks like the sun, and the sun is—what? *The day's eye.* So people called the flower a day's eye, until, eventually, the words fused together: daisy."

At the time, the Australian assumed this was a lie. Now he wonders whether it might be true. Other supposed lies come back to him, some of them assured falsehoods—for example, that dancing thirty minutes per week increases one's life expectancy by upwards of a decade. That one can survive an elevator falling many stories down a shaft by jumping at the exactly the right moment. That the healthiest diet for a human being is comprised of a sweet potato and tofu stir-fry, twelve green leaves, one avocado, an orange, and a handful of Swedish Fish gummies per day, which, when Fiona reported this, happened to describe her own diet exactly. He remembers the lie about albino pigeons with iridescent wings—"like gasoline spilled on the sidewalk," Fiona had said. "That crazy chemical rainbow, which is almost better than the real thing." One after the other, the Australian remembers Fiona's lies. They rush at him, wash over him, the truth or falsehood of each one mattering less and less—and in this moment, standing beside Fiona at their son's birthday party, the Australian falls in love with her, honestly and fully, and he knows it is far too late.

———

The next morning, the Australian takes Maximus for a walk. As they stroll hand in hand down Central Park East, the Australian tells his son that he's going on a trip, a special journey.

"Like a quest?" says Maximus, squinting up through the sunlight at his father.

"Yes, exactly," says the Australian.

"Are you looking for treasure, or are you hunting a bad guy?" Maximus drops his father's hand. He stops walking and peers up at his father.

"Are those the only choices?" asks the Australian.

"Yes," says Maximus. "That's what quests are for. You get treasure or you get the bad guy."

"OK," says the Australian. "I'm on a quest, but I'm not trying to get a bad guy, because there isn't one. Actually, I'm trying to track down a good guy."

"Why?" Maximus stands on his tiptoes, which he does whenever his interest is piqued.

"Well, one day I'm going to come back to New York City, and I'm going to bring the good guy with me."

"Where is he hiding, though?"

"I don't know," says the Australian. "So, it might take a while."

Maximus's face falls. His lower lip begins to tremble.

"I'll be back for Christmas," the Australian quickly, but already Maximus is crying. "Hey." He pulls his son's chin up in order to make eye contact. "It's not forever. Just for a bit. Okay?"

Maximus nods, then pulls his chin from his father's hand and stares down at the pavement. He refuses to continue walking, and the Australian must carry him back to the pop star's mansion.

When the Australian rings the buzzer, Fiona opens the door with a neutral expression on her face. Maximus runs into the parlor to hide amongst his games and toys, and the Australian and Fiona stand facing one another. He wants to tell her he loves her now, in a way that is sane and firm. That he has said the words "I love you" before, but if he said them now they would be real. He loves her as a human being—a love that feels endless and pure, a love that, even though he must never share it, cleanses him from within. Simultaneously, he is aware that he still doesn't really know her, which somehow makes this new love all the more perfect. He thinks it might be the kind of love that a saint feels for all of humanity, or a leper feels for his healer, or a dancing cobra feels for song—the force that compels the snake to uncoil, rise up from its basket, and dance. The Australian knows that if he says "I love you" now, he would mean it, but he also knows that it would be cruel. The kind of love he has to give is not the kind Fiona deserves.

He takes off his backpack, drops it on the floor, and unzips it. From within it, he removes a stack of *Australian Geographic Outdoor* magazines and the manila envelope containing the photograph of Lock Jones. He tells Fiona that they are for Maximus, but he also hopes they are for her, that maybe she might want to see some of the distant lands where, soon, he will be.

The Australian has maintained friendships with Celeste, William, and the boys since moving out of the loft, but the family is presently on a humanitarian trip to Malawi, so he does not have a chance to say goodbye. He mails them a farewell letter, which reads:

I've finally given my heart a vehicle—an airplane, actually. Probably loads of airplanes, maybe some buses and kayaks, too. I'll be doing some traveling. I'm going to live beyond my mind. Thanks for everything and everything else.

Next, the Australian bids farewell to Finn and Vivian.

"This all seems really crazy," says Finn, sitting across from the Australian at a fondue restaurant in Midtown, dark and filled with businessmen. "How did you break it to Maximus?"

"I told him the truth," says the Australian. "At least, the part he can understand. So many people think I'm doing the wrong thing. I just feel like—this is really hard, guys. I want to do the right thing, and I'm being humiliated by everyone I try to talk to."

"No, not at all," says Vivian. "Do you know what the difference is between humiliation and humility?"

"Humiliation is a form of severe embarrassment," he says. "It's shame and self-loathing."

"Exactly," says Vivian. "It can be an indulgence, letting yourself feel that bad. If you are humiliated, all you can think about is that feeling, and strangely, it frees you from having to take action or make choices."

The Australian thinks for a moment. "I think I do that a lot," he says. "So I suppose humility is when you see yourself clearly. You're just being realistic. Humility is being honest with yourself about who you are—the whole picture, good and bad."

"Yes," says Vivian. "I agree."

"I hope I feel that one day. Humility," says the Australian.

"I'm sure you will," says Vivian. "It can be painful, wonderful, a relief, a nightmare. But it's the truth."

"I just have to face it," he says. He looks at Finn, who smiles back at him.

"Ever since you told us about your big trip," says Vivian, "I've been thinking about this idea, one that I think a lot of Americans have, and Europeans too, probably, or maybe it's a worldwide thing—

this notion of what it means to be Australian. Do you guys know what I'm talking about?"

"No," says Finn.

The Australian shrugs. He is now speaking with Vivian the film-maker, the storyteller.

"There's an idea of this universal Australian guy," she explains. "You could find him in any big city, at any hostel or bar, anywhere in the world—smiling, suntanned, carrying a huge backpack. It's just an idea we have, right? But you are going to live the true story be-yond that idea. Like, we think of the Australian—and it turns out he's you." She plucks a strawberry from a bowl and pops it in her mouth. She chews, swallows. "You're going to have some incredible stories to tell." She smiles at the Australian. "I think your trip is going to be amazing. Promise me something?"

"Sure thing," says the Australian.

"Promise to tell me everything."

As soon as the Australian arrives in Melbourne, he checks in on Deedee. He finds her quite well. Jarringly so, in fact—cheerful and a bit impa-tient with the Australian's concern for her. Throughout their meeting at a café near her flat, she has the air of a very busy person, one who feels a pressing urge to get on with things. It is as if Margaret and her death are obscure memories for Deedee, and the Australian wonders if she might have gone back to drugs. He gladly bids her farewell.

From Melbourne, the Australian sets out to follow the Dreaming Tracks, locations that Aboriginal people say have been shaped and imprinted by mythical personas and spirits who come from the al-ternate dimension where dreams live—a place beyond time or space. The sites along the Dreaming Tracks are believed to be the final stop for all souls before reincarnation. He begins at Arnhem Land in the Northern Territory. There, he learns the story of Barnumbirr—a magical being who flew across all of Australia, naming and creating every animal and plant, and forming the land's curves and slopes, rises and falls. Next, in the Victoria River Valley, he learns of a dreaming spirit known as Walujapi, or "black-headed python," whose slithering carved grooves into cliff faces, and whose buttocks imprinted the land when she sat down to set up camp, an indentation which the Australian can see quite clearly—a wide, rounded imprint in the rock. In the Simpson Desert, he learns of the Native Cat Dreaming Spirits, who are said to have come all the way from the sea and then moved onto the areas surrounding Sydney, joining the portion of the Dreaming Tracks where ridges and crests of soft sandstone form the land and rock faces bear ancient engravings: sacred depictions of people, symbols, and animals, including the now-extinct Tasmanian Tiger—a fearsome mix of wolf and big cat, the largest marsupial known to have ever roamed the Earth.

Six weeks into his journey, in Wollemi National Park—a forest thick with eucalyptus, the scent of which stings refreshingly inside the Australian's nostrils—he thinks of his mother, whose travels stopped just short of this point. Chilly in the shade of the lush green tree boughs, he closes his eyes and transports himself to an imagined desert—the forest's opposite. The heat of the desert floor penetrates the soles of his hiking boots and warms his feet. Flowers are growing up, their stems poking through the hot red sand—and then he imagines the sun setting, and it is night, moonless and chilly. He envisions hundreds of thousands of flowers opening their petals, all the way to the horizon in every direction, blooming together at hyperspeed. The feeling of wonderment incurred by this scene fills the Australian's forehead and expands throughout the dark space behind his closed eyes and then down into his torso, resting finally in the hollow just below his lungs. With each breath, he presses against that sensation of fullness, feels its pressure holding him together. He settles into a kind of prayer, the rhythm of his breathing pushing against the image of those flowers, a devotion to everyone he's every loved: Maximus, Fiona, his friends, his mother, and even his father. He knew from the start that his trip would not have a single destination, but many, and he is certain that this place—what would have been his mother's endpoint, had she completed her journey—is one of them.

By the time the Australian reaches Sumatra, eleven months into his travels, he has already traced his father's path throughout much of Southeast Asia. He visited New York for Christmas, as promised, and signed divorce papers with Fiona. He remained in the city through New Year's, which he celebrated with Finn, Vivian, Laurent, and Michelle. "You've changed," they kept saying. "You're just—different." The Australian couldn't be sure whether it was intended as a compliment or a criticism. He didn't ask because he didn't care. Leaving Maximus again was a heart-wrenching ordeal, both father and son in tears.

Now, here is the Australian at Lake Toba. Standing on the edge of the volcanic opening that encircles the lake, he looks down upon the clear, fresh water. He recalls the history of where he stands, as described in Atlas's book: over seventy thousand years ago, the Toba supervolcano erupted, the largest known incident of its kind in the last twenty-five million years. It changed the climate of the entire planet, resulting in a long volcanic winter. A woman the Australian met at his hostel this morning jokingly warned that the event could reoccur at any time, so he had better be careful. He sits down, letting his feet dangle over the lip of the volcano's crater, and drops a pebble—a pockmarked fragment of black volcanic rock—into the blue lake below. Indigo storm clouds hang low in the sky.

The Australian has the widest view on life he has ever had. He senses he is shedding the burdens of his past—the harms incurred by his father, his own guilt for the father and husband he failed to be—and vitality surges through him. A belief that he will make better choices, for himself and for Maximus, solidifies within him, creating a solid core like magma cooling to rock. Although he doesn't yet know what those choices will be, he can see everything, big and small, in its right size—his triumphs and his misdeeds. He recalls his discussion with Vivian about humility. The Australian focuses on his heartbeat, his breathing. Rain begins to fall, and he makes no effort to shield himself. His clothes grow heavy with moisture, yet rays of sun slice through the storm clouds, glinting on the lake's surface inside the volcano's center.

In this moment, the Australian has a series of revelations. The skin of the person you love will always feel like velvet in the morning. The best kind of euphoria comes as a result of a week's starvation. In old age, shaving reemerges as a life-affirming activity, just as it was in adolescence. All of Fiona's lies, so modest and hopeful, were *possible*. Everything unlikely is, by definition, possible. It is possible to attain a high level of proficiency at a new language at any point in life. It is possible to live in New York City if one breathes from the diaphragm. There may be no such thing as righteousness, but happiness might still be possible. Kindness is possible. Extreme weather is possible. Albino pigeons with iridescent wings are possible. Mercy, redemption, flowers pushing up through red desert sand, blooming purple and white under a starry, moonless sky—all of it is possible.

ACKNOWLEDGMENTS

L ate one night during my second semester of graduate school—
caffeinate-buzzed, my dog Phil sleeping at my feet, avoiding
the stack of essays I should've been grading—I was scrolling
through old story fragments buried in folders within folders on my
laptop and came across a file entitled "The Australian." No bells rung.
I opened it, read the first few sentences, and recalled, with startling
clarity, a sweltering July afternoon in 2001. I was nineteen, had just
bombed out of college, my mind aflame with mania. In a Greenwich
Village café, I struck up a conversation with a savagely handsome
Australian man, about thirty. After lengthy chatter—mostly from
me—I followed him back to his SoHo loft. He'd said he was a venture capitalist and his home's sparse, expensive furnishings seemed
to confirm it: a sleek, black leather couch and glass coffee table, two
skylights, a stainless-steel refrigerator containing nothing but Champagne, and a low-to-the-ground king-size bed in the corner.

The Australian man produced a baggie of crystalline cocaine and
snorted two slim lines from a circle of mirrored glass. I snorted one
fat line and tilted my head back. "Want some water?" he asked, but
before I could respond he kissed me, gently. "Wait!" I said. Without
asking, I popped a Duran Duran cassette into his expensive sound
system, spun up the volume, and began dancing. He watched me

bemusedly for a few songs, then patted a spot on the edge of his bed. I sat, expecting another kiss, too high to know whether I wanted one or not. Instead, he told me stories from his youth in Melbourne. I listened, rapt. Before I left, he removed from one of three tall bookshelves a self-help book—I noticed, then, that *all* his books were of that genre—and slipped it into my ratty messenger bag, saying, "This will change your life."

At home, I withdrew the book from my bag: *Conversations With God* by Neale Donald Walsch. An atheist and disdainful of all things New Age, I was put off by the title, but two pages in I was astonished to find myself mesmerized, filled with a queer kind of hope—ravenous and sincere. That feeling enlarged, page after page. By the end, I was an impassioned believer in a benevolent, all-powerful God, one that could extricate me from the psychotic mania and suicidal depression I'd been looping around since age twelve, release me from drug addiction, and give me a chance at a life in which I could thrive, act with intention, create, speak honestly, love. Twenty-four hours later I was in drug detox, which was followed by five months of rehab in Delray Beach, Florida. With nowhere else to go, I remained in that city for three years, working odd jobs. After taking classes at a local university, I reenrolled at the college I'd first attended, in New York's Hudson Valley, and began writing fiction. I was properly medicated for bipolar disorder. Soon after graduation, I moved to Gainesville to attend the University of Florida's MFA program in creative writing.

The four-page document I found in my computer, written hastily years earlier and immediately forgotten, contained the most memorable details of the Australian man's youth in Melbourne, which he'd shouted over "Girls on Film" and "Electric Barbarella" and "Rio." As I read the pages, I wanted the stories to continue, the life behind them to be made manifest—that this would be my first novel. While my spiritual beliefs no longer derive from *Conversations With God*, the book had come at a moment in which the combination of intoxication and desperation enabled me to believe, for the first time, that I could climb up and out of the hole I had so long been plummeting down. And so, I owe the Australian man, who I knew for just one day, boundless gratitude—for inspiring the character at this novel's center, and also, perhaps, for my life.

There are so many other people to whom I owe this book and the life I have today. I must begin by thanking Sheila Aldendorff, my piano teacher from age five to twelve, who taught me how to be an artist. Thank you to Kara Stern, my beloved high school English teacher, for believing in me as reader and writer despite my colossal struggle, in those years, to make it as a human being—let alone make it to class on time. And I thank Mona Simpson, professor at my alma mater, Bard College, for her mentorship and for welcoming me into the fold of writers.

I am forever indebted to the faculty of MF@FLA—my mentors Jill Ciment, Michael Hofmann, David Leavitt, Padgett Powell, and Mary Robison—for their guidance, thoughtful criticism, and encouragement. I am also hugely grateful to my cohort in the program, whose own stories and novels taught me so much, and who saw the beginning pages of this novel and assured me, "Yes, it's a book." In particular, the editorial feedback I received from Liz Bevilacqua, Becca Evanhoe, RL Goldberg, Heather Peterson, Amy Scharmann, and Sarah Trudgeon was transformative. Also among this group was Travis Fristoe, whose warmth, generosity, and enthusiasm motivated me through rough patches of writing and life. His death in August of 2015 left a hole in a world that needs him.

I am also deeply thankful to Benjy Caplan, Tim Horvath, and Mark Mitchell, each of whom read the manuscript and offered not only sage writing advice but buoyed my spirits as I entered into the phase of seeking a publisher. Fortunately that quest was undertaken with my brilliant agent, Kristyn Keene, strong at the helm. I first met her when I was about fifteen pages into writing the book, and she stuck with me—very, very patiently—for the next several years as I finished it. It is because of Kristyn's positivity, wisdom, and savvy that Dzanc Books became the publisher of *The Australian* and my forthcoming story collection, *Greyhounds*—and I cannot imagine any better home for both books.

My editor, Dzanc Books' editor-in-chief, Guy Intoci, may be in possession of supernatural powers—something like laser beams that shoot from his eyes, outlining the necessary pages I neglected to write and illuminating the bits that had to go. His vision and excitement helped me shape and strengthen the novel immeasurably. I also owe much gratitude to Michelle Dotter, senior editor, for her sharp and insightful edits, and to Michael Seidlinger, director of publicity, who has worked tirelessly on behalf of this novel.

I am immensely fortunate to have friends who are family—not by blood, but something just as vital. Many are people who met me when I had just learned to survive, and all taught me how to live. Thank you Liz Bevilacqua, Andrew Donovan, Becca Evanhoe, Sally Greenberg, RL Goldberg, Matt Griepp, Carrie Guss, Ruth McGregor Hamann, Mia Lipton, Heather Peterson, Mike Quinn, Amy Scharmann, Rachel Shepherd, and Molly Williams.

None of my life—let alone the writing of this book—would have been possible without the extraordinary love and support of my mother, Rebecca Smith, and my father, Peter Stevens. They have been there for me in every conceivable way, and no words can capture the gratitude their love and support inspires in me. I am also beyond fortunate to have three amazing brothers with whom I share unconditional love and camaraderie: Sam Smith-Stevens, Luke Smith-Stevens, and Oliver Stevens. Each of them shines uniquely—all equally bright. I thank my grandmother, Debby Stevens, for her stories and love; my stepparents, Simona Stevens and Michael Coffey, for each of their loving support; and my aunt and uncle, Jamie and Aaron Renning, for their love, friendship, sanity, and unparalleled sense of humor.

This book is dedicated to my husband, Sebastian Boensch, whose love is the greatest gift of my life. Through the way he speaks to me and touches me, the interactions I witness between him and others— and even the way he cares for our dear dogs, Phil and Potter—he exemplifies kindness, patience, affection, sincerity, and compassion. He is unwavering and strong in his loyalty and support, a truly good human being, singularly gifted writer, and devoted partner. All that he is inspires the best in me.